The Order

Donald Cimmino

The Order

Vanguard Press

A CIP catalogue record for this title is
available from the British Library.

ISBN 978 1 83794 186 5

This is a work of fiction. Names, characters, businesses, places, events
and incidents are either the product of the author's imagination or used
in a fictitious manner. Any resemblance to actual persons, living or
dead, or actual events is purely coincidental.

*Vanguard Press is an imprint of
Pegasus Elliot Mackenzie Publishers Ltd.*
www.pegasuspublishers.com

First Published in 2024

**Vanguard Press
Sheraton House Castle Park
Cambridge England**

Printed & Bound in Great Britain

Introduction

As the inhabitants of the planets within the Stasia Galaxy began to develop their technologies, they began to interact with other planets within the galaxy. Out of this interaction, a number of trade alliances grew and prospered. This led to the eventual formation of small federations throughout the galaxy. Power struggles between federations became common as they began to expand their activities. Certain federations embarked on a quest to establish supremacy and to build an empire. Two large federations emerged as supreme within the galaxy. The Borian Federation and the Lexiconian Federation began colonizing throughout the galaxy. They were unable to coexist peacefully for very long. A galactic war resulted from which one federation would gain sole control of the galaxy. The long and very destructive war came to an end when the main Borian fleet was mysteriously destroyed while amassing for a major offensive near the planet Vendra. The loss was so devastating that Boriah surrendered to Lexicon and Stasia was united when Lexicon formed an empire known as The Realm.

The capital of The Realm was established on the planet Lexicon and the central government operated from there. It consisted of the Director and the Council. The Director was the most powerful politician in The Realm and acted with the power of an emperor. The Council was made up of other powerful politicians who benefited from the actions of the Director. All interplanetary activities were governed by Realm law. Each planet had its own set of local laws but they had to fit into the structure of Realm law or they would not be recognized as legally binding.

The Stasia Galaxy has prospered for millennia under The Realm but the political situation is becoming contentious and signs of a power struggle are beginning to emerge. The prosperity was due to the ability of The Realm to tap into the resources within the galaxy. But now that those resources are becoming exhausted, and economic growth has flattened, the Director's ability is being challenged. Although he still has control, there are other powerful councilmen who are beginning to gather support for a challenge. No director has ever been removed from his position in the past. They have all governed until retirement or death. As long as The Realm continues to prosper, there will be no challenge. But as all things must end, so the times of effortless prosperity have come to an end for The Realm. The Director must devise a plan to restore economic growth or face the eventual challenge that will force him from power.

Chapter 1

Business As Usual

Ruther grumbles, "This galaxy has been peaceful for too long. There hasn't been a war in centuries. How can a private trader make any notes in a galaxy like this? It is always good when the galaxy is divided. It creates a lot of opportunities with the warrin' factions tryin' to cut off each other's trade. There's a lot of notes to be made in smugglin'. Fast notes. Can't get used to this tradin' under The Realm. You either have to be a member of the commercial fleet and work for the government or settle for the crumbs like we're doin'."

Laar fires back, "At least we can come and go as we please. One of these days we'll come up with something that the fleet hasn't already bought into."

Ruther continues. "Where? They have this galaxy sewn up. We get to trade with the planets that The Realm doesn't want to be bothered with. And they don't have any notes. We're starvin'."

Laar snaps, "Oh, it isn't that bad. We still have one of the best vessels in the galaxy. We can get to any place that we need to."

Ruther answers sarcastically, "Yeah, and if The Realm wants it, we won't have it for long. And if we start makin' notes, they'll want it."

Laar changes the subject. "Meris is only a few light-minutes away."

"Then slow this vessel down", Ruther says. "I'm in no hurry to get there. We'll land, trade enough farmin' hardware to replenish our food and fuel supplies, and hope that a few of those farmers want some luxury items so that we can have a few notes in our pockets to cut loose with when we get back to civilization. It's the same old routine."

Laar states, "We get by, and underneath all of your complaining, you know that you enjoy this life as much as I do."

Ruther responds, "With a few more notes I could enjoy it a whole lot more."

Laar again changes the subject. "We're entering the atmosphere. It will take us a few planetary-hours to get down. Get yourself together while you have the time."

Casually Ruther says, "What's to prepare? I'm already bored to death. There's nothin' special down there that I haven't seen a hundred times before."

Laar responds, "Well, I'm going to rest up."

Ruther bellows, "What in stars do you need to rest up for? We're just goin' to sell some tools."

Laar answers immediately, "But I'm the one who has to load them all. The stars would go cold before you gave me any help."

Ruther answers sarcastically, "Well, if I'm goin' to unload the stuff, what would I need you for?"

Laar says offhandedly, "Make your jokes. I'm not even listening."

Ruther gets serious. "You know you spoke of the stars goin' cold. Those damn dead solar systems really have me thinkin'."

Laar inquires, "Thinking of what?"

Ruther, still serious, says, "Thinkin' of what the damn things are all about."

Laar continues, "There are hundreds of them all over the universe. Which ones are you so curious about?"

Ruther is still serious. "The ones that have been around for billions of years don't concern me. But I've been noticing the ones in the Cotalion Galaxy. It seems to be happenin' at a pretty steady rate there, and all in the same vicinity. I wonder what's goin' on?"

Laar says jokingly, "You're not going to find any fun times in a dead solar system and that's all you have ever thought about before. There's no life at all there. Once the suns went cold, whatever was on those planets, if anything, isn't there anymore."

Ruther says sternly, "I'd like to know what caused those suns to burn out. It's not normal."

Laar says, "It happens."

Annoyed, Ruther says, "But it never happened in my lifetime before. Now all of a sudden a bunch of them spring up. Somethin' isn't right."

Laar cuts in. "We're getting our landing instructions, Ruther. Prepare for a landing."

Surprised, Ruther says, "Here already? Oh well."

From Meris comes the message: "This is Meris air traffic control. You are to identify now."

Laar answers, "This is private trade vessel *Ibex*."

Cholly from Meris says, "Hello, Laar! Back to stock up again?"

Laar asks, "Is that you Cholly?"

Cholly answers, "It's me."

Laar says cheerfully, "It's good to be landed by a friend for a change. The last few times they shoved us into real holes. If you aren't a Realm ship, they don't treat you real nice around here."

Cholly reassures Laar, "Don't worry, Laar. Head for port three. I'll send you a beam. It's a good one."

Laar says, "Thanks, Cholly."

Cholly asks, "Say, Laar, are you going to be here for a while this time?"

Laar replies, "No. It's the usual trade and run for us."

Cholly inquires, "Where's that grouch, Ruther? Maybe I can talk him into having a drink or two before you leave. I haven't seen either one of you in a while. You guys show up here at least twice a month, but you never stop in on me."

Laar says, "I always try to talk Ruther into going to see you, but he's always in a hurry to get back to his hot spots and spend his notes on a good time. He has a couple of places that he frequents."

Cholly says sarcastically, "I can just imagine what they're like."

Laar says, "Let me get Ruther. Hey, Ruther! Cholly is landing us. He wants to talk to you."

Ruther says excitedly says, "Cholly old buddy, are you givin us a good port?"

Cholly answers jokingly, "I should put you in a hole somewhere, you old grouch. You never stop by anymore."

Ruther says, "You know how it is, Cholly. This place doesn't do anythin' for me. Why don't you put in for a transfer?"

Cholly responds, "I have some close friends here, Ruther. I don't want to leave this place."

Ruther jokes, "You mean you have a woman?"

Cholly ignores him. "Why don't you and Laar have a few drinks with me before you leave?"

Ruther gives in. "All right, Cholly. Where do we meet you?"

Cholly states, "I'm landing you at port three. Right in the area there's a place called A Piece of Paradise. Just ask anybody. They'll tell you how to get there. I'd better get off the frequency. See you later."

Laar says, "I'm looking forward to seeing Cholly again, Ruther."

Ruther says, "Me too. We used to have a good time at the academy together."

Laar says, "Well, we're in. Let's make our connections. The sooner we finish our business, the sooner we'll see Cholly."

Ruther states, "I'll do the callin', you get the inventory and ledgers ready."

Laar answers sarcastically, "As usual."

***

Ruther states, "Pretty good trip this time, Laar. We must have hit a good time for these farmers. We sold a lot of trinkets this trip."

Laar agrees. "Maybe we should stock up on a few more expensive items next time we come here. It looks like they were ready to spend. If we had the right stuff on hand, we could have made a lot of notes."

Ruther says, "I wonder why the big change. Never knew these farmers to be like this before."

Laar guesses, "Maybe Cholly knows something."

Ruther adds, "Yeah, we'll ask him. Now what was the name of that place that he mentioned?"

Laar answers, "A Piece of Paradise."

Ruther quips, "That's it. We'd better ask somebody where it is".

Ruther inquires, "Hey, friend! Can you tell us where we can find A Piece of Paradise?"

Stranger says, "Not on this planet."

Ruther continues, "We were told that it is not far from here."

The stranger answers, "Oh, you mean the inn. I thought you were some sort of religious fanatics from off planet looking for a place to settle. I never go there myself, but it's just around the corner."

Ruther replies, "Thanks, friend. Let's go, Laar. I'm ready for a few."

Laar says sarcastically, "That's nothing new."

Ruther says, surprised, "Hey! This place is mobbed. How in stars are we goin' to find Cholly in here?"

Laar says, "Let's look around."

Ruther stares. "Look at that bar. It's packed. I'll die of thirst before I get near it."

Laar quips, "You'll manage. Why don't you work your way up there and I'll look for Cholly. When I find him, I'll come back and get you."

Ruther adds, "Good idea. But you mean if you find him. I might never see you again once we separate."

Laar starts away. "I'll see you later, Ruther."

Ruther shouts, "Hey, beautiful! Do you work here?"

The cocktail waitress answers, "Yes. What do you need, stranger?"

Ruther asks, "Can you fix me up with a drink?"

The cocktail waitress replies, "I can fix you up with more than that if you want it."

Ruther says to himself, *Hey, this place sounds real friendly. I wonder why I never heard of it before.*

The cocktail waitress asks, "Don't you have any friends on this planet?"

Ruther answers, "Yeah, that's who told me about it. Say! Maybe you know my friend. He's supposed to be here and without some help, I don't think I'll ever find him. His name is Cholly."

The cocktail waitress asks, "Cholly the lander?"

Ruther answers, "Yeah. So, you know him?"

The waitress says, "He's always in here with his friends. All the landers hang out here. They hang out in those terraced off rooms to the left of the bar."

Ruther says, "Thanks. You've been a lot of help. How about that drink? After I find my friend, maybe you can get me more than a drink."

The waitress states, "Better hurry, stranger. I make friends fast."

Ruther counters, "I bet you do. See you later, beautiful."

Ruther says to himself, *Now where is Laar? First I guess I'll try to find Cholly. Then I'll worry about Laar.*

Laar shouts, "Ruther!"

Ruther yells back, "Hey! I know where Cholly hangs out."

Laar says, "I already found him. He's right over there."

Ruther gestures. "Well, let's go. I still need a drink. Hey! You should see the beauty I just met while I was goin' up to the bar. And I didn't forget about my drink. She told me where Cholly hangs out and I was on my way over."

Laar points, "There he is."

Ruther says excitedly, "Hey, Cholly! Long time no see!"

Cholly says, "You still look the same, Ruther. Don't you ever change? Meet my buddies. They are fellow landers. Guys, this is Ruther. We go way back."

Ruther mutters, "I hope they're not the guys that have been puttin' us in those holes every time we land here.

Cholly says, "Guys, Ruther is an old friend from the academy. One of my closest."

Ruther interrupts. "Say, Cholly, can you get me a drink? I was almost up to the bar when I got to talkin' to some girl. You must know her. She told me where you hang out."

Cholly answers, "Must have been one of the girls who work here."

Ruther says, "Yeah. Say, how do they operate here? She was awful friendly."

Cholly replies, "That's how they operate. They're real charmers until you run out of notes. But business is business. You know how it is."

Ruther inquires, "So, what have you been up to? It's no wonder why you don't want a transfer. I didn't think this planet had anythin' like this to offer. This is a great hangout."

Cholly states nonchalantly, "I just come here after work to wind down a bit."

Ruther replies, "This place winds me up. Say, Cholly, I've been meanin' to ask you, what in stars is happenin' here? This place has changed all of a sudden. The farmers seem to have more notes, there seem to be more off worlders here, and hangouts like this. I don't get it."

Cholly replies, "Things are going to change even more by the time you make your next trip here. Cotalion has become interested in trading with this planet on full scale."

Ruther says with surprise, "Cotalion? And The Realm is lettin' them in? I wonder why? The Realm usually doesn't take kindly to competition. I think it's time for me to find a new planet to do business on. Things will probably get real hot around here pretty soon."

Cholly replies, "I don't know, Ruther. They've been keeping a close watch on the Cotalion ships, but they haven't done anything to stop them."

Ruther mutters, "I guess I won't be able to afford to trade here anymore. And that answers my question about the farmers bein' willin' to buy all those trinkets we sold."

Laar says, "You must be pretty busy now, Cholly."

Cholly replies, "They're bringing in more landers to handle the increased traffic. They will be building some new ports too."

Ruther asks, "Are they invitin' these guys in? What's up?"

Cholly says, "Beats me. But things are getting a lot better around here since this Cotalion trade began. We are a major trading planet again."

Ruther asks, "What do we have that they want so badly?"

Cholly answers, "Food."

Ruther asks, "Food? Why do they need our galaxy to supply them with food? Is their population on the rise, or did they suffer a famine of some sort?"

Cholly asks, "Have you noticed the dead systems in Cotalion?"

Ruther replies, "Funny thing but me and Laar were just talkin' about that before we landed."

Cholly informs him, "Well, those systems contained some of the most fertile and productive farm planets in Cotalion. Until they can adjust to the loss, they will need food from us."

Ruther says, "But they are pushin' The Realm."

Laar interrupts. "Well, you wanted to see a war so that we could make some easy notes. Maybe you'll get your wish."

Ruther answers, "Yeah, but not a war with another galaxy, Laar. We might lose and there's no notes for a loser. They might even confiscate our vessel."

Laar counters, "Take it easy. We haven't even gone to war let alone lost."

Ruther adds, "If there is a war with another galaxy, The Realm may very well confiscate every useful ship they can find. I wanted a little conflict within Stasia. That's where the notes can be made. I don't want an inter-galactic war. Maybe we'd better get out of this galaxy and head for a neutral one before we're unable to leave."

Laar replies, "Hold on, Ruther! You're in a panic over nothing. Besides, you've never been outside of Stasia. Chances are we won't even be welcome somewhere else.

We might get in a worse jam if we are mistaken for invaders."

Ruther says, "We don't have any Realm markin'. We're neutral. Private traders."

Laar points out, "If The Realm goes to war, you can be sure that they'll examine the possibilities of victory before they do."

Ruther fires back, "Don't you think that Cotalion has made some calculations too?"

Laar says, "They have no choice. They need food. No matter what they calculate, they must take the chance."

Ruther asks, "Has Cotalion tried to contact The Realm Council yet?"

Cholly responds, "Not as far as I know."

Ruther asks, "Then why doesn't the Council forbid trade with the Cotalions?"

Cholly answers, "I guess they're afraid that if the Cotalions were prevented from trading, they may be forced to take what they need. The Council doesn't like being forced into making a move until they are fully prepared. So, in the meantime they have gone out of their way to avoid a conflict with the Cotalions. The Fleet has even begun to trade with planets that they formerly chose not to deal with in order to stay clear of them."

Ruther grumbles, "There goes the rest of our trade. I came in here to talk over old times and have a few laughs and look at how it turned out."

Cholly says apologetically, "Sorry, Ruther. But at least you know what is going on now. Why don't we forget about it and have a good time like you had planned in the first place. I'll order us another round."

Chapter 2

The Realm

The Director speaks. "I have called you all here to ensure that there is no blunder. You have already alerted me on several occasions to the fact that the Cotalions have been trading in the sectors nearest their galaxy and that they have been trying to contact you. I gave you an order that all trade by the Commercial Fleet is to be diverted in a fashion to prevent interference with the Cotalion trade. I also ordered you not to contact the Cotalions under any circumstances. Why do you insist on questioning my orders? Don't you believe that I am capable of controlling this empire?"

A councilman replies, "We just believe that if we contact the Cotalions, we can make a trade agreement with them and avoid a possible incident."

The Director states, "You are all fine bureaucrats but poor strategists. If we make a trade agreement, we will be bound to a fixed exchange rate. The Realm is making a fortune on this open trade. They are forcing up the exchange rate every day due to their overwhelming demand. They are desperate for the food so they must accept any price that is asked."

Another councilman replies, "But if the rates go too high, I'm afraid that they will begin to take what they need by force. Then we will be faced with war."

The Director replies angrily, "You fools! They can't take the chance of starting a war because if they did their food source will be cut off. They must have the food. If they get their supply cut off, they will defeat their own purpose. This is the opportunity of a lifetime. The Realm has been prospering for a long time but at a steadily declining rate. We are at the point where further growth within Stasia is at a standstill. The Realm has tapped every viable source of wealth within the galaxy. We have been able to maintain our present level of prosperity but unable to increase it. Now with the Cotalion trade, we have found a new source of wealth to tap. Why should we limit ourselves by entering into a trade agreement? We will absorb as much of Cotalions' wealth as we can. You will not ruin this opportunity. You will continue to obey my orders until I tell you otherwise. Do you understand?"

In unison the Council replies, "Yes, Director."

The Director continues, "Now that that is settled, I would like a report on the status of your particular areas of responsibility. Setting aside the Cotalion trade, give me a report on commerce."

The Commerce Manager reports, "All trade is being carried on throughout Stasia in an orderly and efficient manner. No unregistered vessels have operated in any of the commercial sectors. The Realm Commercial Fleet has been increased by seven major cargo vessels and thirteen shuttles since last meeting. Private trade vessels have not been permitted to affiliate and six vessels were confiscated and added to the Fleet for violation of the Non-Affiliation Act. We are making excellent progress toward the completion of new landing ports on all agricultural trading planets within fifty light-days of the Cotalion/Stasia border zone. There has been no disruption of inter-planetary travel within Stasia except for three reported acts of piracy, all of which are being investigated presently. All communications between planets and The Realm capital remain intact. Nothing unusual to report."

The Director continues, "Good. Now give me a report on industry and agriculture."

The Agricultural Manager reports, "Agricultural efforts have been intensified to meet the new demand created by the Cotalion trade. Output has not yet increased but projections show that an increase of three to six percent can be expected by next quarter. Manufacture of metal products has been shifted from less essential areas to the manufacture of farming implements and machinery at a rate shift of eight percent. This should be more than adequate to support the increased farming effort. Mining is at a level equal to manufacturing demand. No shortages have been reported by any planet. New mines are being planned for planets seven, eight, and nine of the Pallus System in Sector 6C. This is tied into future plans for industrial expansion. All other industries remain unchanged."

The Director continues, "Good. Now give me a report on finance."

The Finance Manager reports, "An adequate note supply is available in all sectors to support day-to-day transactions. We have a surplus due to a decrease in borrowing by the planetary governments. All planets remain solvent. Realm assets have increased by approximately seven billion notes value due mainly to the food trade with Cotalion."

The Director crows, "Excellent! When was the last time we had an increase like that? And you want a trade agreement." The Director continues, "I need a report on our security status."

The Head of Security reports, "All bases are on full alert status and are reported battle ready. There have been no incidents of internal unrest, so I must conclude that The Realm is secure. However, the crime rate is up slightly due to increased pirate activity. When we shifted those patrols to watch the Cotalions, we left an opening for the pirates. It doesn't take them long to take advantage of a situation. The Cotalion trade has had an effect on public opinion. There is some speculation and a lot of rumors circulating around the galaxy. A feeling of uncertainty is beginning to spread. That is not a healthy situation."

The Director answers, "I will handle public opinion by releasing news that The Realm and Cotalion are in the process of negotiations and that in the interim, Cotalion vessels are being permitted to trade under our constant military supervision. Such a report is not entirely untrue and it should ease the controversy. Meanwhile, you will make certain that the Cotalion trade is monitored and you will report to me daily regarding all Cotalion activity within Stasia. You are not to act without my direct order. Just report! Is that understood?"

The Head of Security continues, "Our police have been alerted to the fact that piracy may increase until an example is made of our ability to thwart their attempts. I am authorizing a joint effort between police and the military to handle the pirates. Upon request, the military will supply support to any police action. Military patrols will be mobilized so that at any given time, there will be the availability of an already spaceborne detachment ready to assist without delay. The pirates will not be able to exist in such a climate."

The director concludes, "Now that the reports are concluded, here is my order. In the eventuality that Cotalion attempts to expand trade too deep into Stasia, or if they attempt aggression, we will increase our production of weapons by twenty percent immediately. The military will be obliged to conduct an adequate amount of maneuvers to ensure their battle readiness.

"Is there any other business that you wish to discuss before we adjourn? Very well. This meeting is adjourned. Refreshments will be provided if desired, but I must leave. I have some pressing business to attend to."

***

The director commands, "Attendant! Summon the chief of intelligence to the viewer."

The chief of intelligence answers, "This is Brodis replying to your summons."

The director orders, "Brodis, come to the palace at once."

The chief of intelligence replies, "Yes, Director. Immediately!"

The Director orders, "Attendant, take me back to the palace. Upon our arrival, prepare the study with proper refreshments for a lengthy meeting for two. Also have two of my mistresses readied for call."

The ttendant informs him, "Brodis has arrived."

Brodis asks, "What is your wish, Director?"

The Director says, "Be seated, Brodis. We have much to discuss. Care for some vintaged laca?"

Brodis replies enthusiastically, "Yes, indeed, sir."

The Director says, "You'll have to pour your own. I don't want any servants around to hear our discussion. Let's get down to business. You've done an excellent job of detonating those suns without being detected."

Brodis states, "With the use of this new device, detection is almost impossible."

The Director replies, "True. But the trick was in planting the device without being detected. You did that nine times. Now my plan is in full swing and it is paying off handsomely. My scientists are working on new weapons all the time."

Brodis asks, "What else could you possibly need? This new device is super."

The Director replies, "I need better methods of delivery. I want to expand its range. Make it a multiple target weapon if possible. Remember, Brodis, you must always seek to improve things. Satisfaction leads to submission and The Realm does not submit."

Brodis agrees. "Right you are, sir."

The Director informs him, "So far, we have created nine dead systems within Cotalion. Those nine systems that we extinguished were the major food suppliers for about one tenth of the entire Cotalion Galaxy. That set up the food trade that Cotalion has undertaken with our outer agricultural planets. They are desperate for food and we are making a fortune supplying it. My plan is working to perfection but if they ever find out the reason why their systems went dead, it would be war. We must make sure they never discover our actions. We must also keep this trade flourishing. I'm sure they are taking steps to remedy the present situation. We must make sure that they are unable to get back on their feet again. I don't want to use the device again unless I must. It would be safer if we can find a method to disrupt their attempts to rebuild their farming capacity. That is your task, Brodis. You must devise a way to infiltrate and disrupt the Cotalions."

Brodis assures him, "I will find a way, sir."

The Director inquires, "Good. Have you been able to find out anything about the Septis Galaxy?"

Brodis answers, "The only thing I know is that they will not allow a Cotalion vessel, or for that matter, one of ours, to enter their space. I have sent spies, but they never made it through the border zone."

The Director says, "I had hoped to do to Septis what we have done to Cotalion, but we will forget about Septis for now. As long as they are no threat to us, they are of little consequence. For now you are to concentrate on Cotalion. That is your assignment."

Brodis replies, "I will carry out your command. As soon as I formulate a plan, I will report back to you."

The Director states, "Good. I don't think that we have any more business to discuss. Attendant! Send in the mistresses. You will stay for a while, won't you?

Brodis replies enthusiastically, "Of course, sir. You know how much I enjoy your hospitality."

Chapter 3

A New Venture

Ruther says, "Laar, I think I just found a way to make some big notes."

Laar asks, "How is that, Ruther?"

Ruther replies, "This Cotalion thing. They need food. We have a transport vessel. We can buy a load of food and sell it to Cotalion. They're payin' high prices for food. What do you think?"

Laar says, "I think it's easier said than done."

Ruther continues, "We're at opportunity's door. All we have to do is walk in and take all we can get. We may never get a chance like this again."

Laar replies, "You're a dreamer. We can't just walk up to the Cotalions and sell them food. The Realm would have something to say about that. We won't be able to get near them."

Ruther says, "We'll deliver the food right to them."

Laar says with surprise, "You don't mean into Cotalion?"

Ruther answers, "Why not?"

Laar says with disbelief, "Are you crazy? We'll never get past the border patrols. Or did you forget that The Realm forbids any vessel from leaving Stasia."

Ruther says with conviction, "We can do it. They won't expect anyone to try. We'll surprise them and be across before they can react."

Laar replies with skepticism, "Even if we did make it into Cotalion, which is unlikely, we might be taken for invaders. They might blast us right out of space. We would be helpless. Our ship isn't built for speed or maneuverability."

Ruther counters, "Come on, Laar. Why would they attack a lone vessel? Especially a transport. They might force us down or board us, but when they see that we are loaded with food, they'll welcome us with open arms."

Laar adds, "They might also confiscate our vessel and throw us into some prison, if they don't kill us first."

Ruther continues, "Not if we tell them that we'll bring them more next trip. We'll undersell The Realm. They'll be happy to do business with us. Besides, what choice do we have? With The Realm movin' in on our normal trade spots, we'll have to settle for whatever scraps are left."

Laar says, "We could find other sources."

Ruther exclaims, "That's just it, Laar. We've just found one. Cotalion. We can get gems and metals and who knows what else for our food and sell them for big notes here in Stasia. No more sellin trinkets to people on desolate planets for a few notes. Big notes, Laar! After a few shipments, we may even be able to buy our own port space in the capital."

Laar says with skepticism, "I'll believe it when I see it."

Ruther inquires, "Then you agree to try?"

Laar states, "You would do it whether I agree or not, so I'll make it easier for both of us."

Ruther exclaims, "You just made the best decision of your life, next to becomin' my shipmate."

Laar snaps, "You mean your partner."

Ruther answers, "Same thing. Shipmate just sounds friendlier. Let's drink to our new enterprise."

***

Laar observes, "I didn't think you'd ever wake up, Ruther."

Ruther asks drowsily, "Am I awake? I think I drank too much."

Laar responds, "You always drink too much."

Ruther answers jokingly, "Is that any way to talk to a man with a headache?"

Laar asks, "Are you in any shape to discuss our trading plans with Cotalion?"

Ruther answers, "I can talk."

Laar asks, "Have you decided where we will be buying the food?"

Ruther replies, "First of all, we have to decide what we want to transport. I think that we should try to carry somethin' that isn't too bulky so that we can carry a lot of it. We want to make the most out of this trip."

Laar thinks, "Grain probably packs the best, but it won't be worth as much as meat, fruit, or vegetables."

Ruther adds, "Maybe that dehydrated stuff. That way we can carry the expensive stuff and it will be compact and lightweight."

Laar agrees, "Great idea, Ruther! We'll be able to carry a lot and still be selling the higher priced items. We can buy at process planet Ura. It's only about ten l-days from the Cotalion border in Sector C9. It'll only take us six l-days to get there from here. That isn't far at all."

Ruther suggests, "I suggest that we stop off at Lexicon for a few days and have a little fun before we head for the unknown. We may not have a chance to unwind for a long time once we get under way."

Laar quips, "Pleasure before business, right, Ruther."

Ruther urges, "Come on."

Laar submits. "All right, let's go."

Ruther adds, "I've got a couple of girls waitin' for me from the last time I was there."

Laar asks, "How do you know that they are still waiting?"

Ruther counters, "That's what they're there for, Laar."

***

Laar exclaims, "It's about time you came back. I guess you found those girls you spoke about."

Ruther answers, "They were waitin'. The only reason I'm back this soon is that I ran out of notes."

Laar says sarcastically, "This soon? You've been gone four days. Too bad you blew all your notes."

Ruther exclaims, "It was worth it. These girls are fantastic. They give you a time you never forget. What did you do with your time?"

Laar answers, "I enjoyed the beaches during the day and took in the shows at night."

Ruther inquires, "You didn't have any girls?"

Laar answers, "I met a lot of them on the beach. I took a couple of them out to dinner and a show."

Ruther further inquires, "You didn't spend a night with any?"

Laar answers, "I spent the night with one."

Ruther says sarcastically, "That's a relief. I thought you might have lost your manhood somewhere."

Laar states, "We have to get going. I heard that Cotalion has been trading on Ura. We may not be able to buy there because their production is already bought up. They just can't keep up with the demand created by the Cotalion traders."

Ruther replies, "That's nonsense. If we show our notes, they'll sell us the food."

Laar responds, "I hope you're right, Ruther."

Ruther says, "Well let's get goin'. I'm out of notes anyway. The only way to get more is to get to work. Get us clearance and we'll leave."

***

Laar states, "We're approaching Ura."

Ruther asks, "How close are we?"

Laar answers, "We'll be in their atmosphere in half an l-hour."

Ruther suggests, "Let's eat somethin' before we get landin' instructions."

Laar adds, "All right, but go easy on the alcohol. We have to deal once we land."

Ruther exclaims, "You leave the dealin' to me."

Laar advises, "We're entering the atmosphere. I'm going to get landing instructions. This is *Ibex* to Landing Control. Request landing instructions."

Landing Control demands, "State your purpose, *Ibex*."

Laar replies, "We want to buy food and refuel."

Landing Control responds, "You're wasting your time if you want to buy food, but I'll land you if you so desire."

Laar asks, "Did you hear that, Ruther?"

Ruther says, "No. What did he say?"

Laar repeats, "He says that we are wasting our time if we want to buy food."

Ruther says, "Let's go down, Laar."

Laar advises, "Landing Control, we wish to land."

Landing Control responds, "Set your course to SW47. You'll be landing in port 26. You'll just be a short shuttle ride from brokers' offices."

Laar acknowledges, "Thanks. *Ibex* out. Now what, Ruther?"

Ruther snaps, "Now we buy some food."

Laar says, "You heard the lander."

Ruther continues, "What does a lander know? Just take us down."

Laar advises, "We'll be down in ten minutes."

Ruther says, "I guess I'll put my boots on."

Laar states, "We're in."

Ruther says, "Good. You prepare the storage areas. I have some dealin' to do. If I'm not back in seven hours, come and get me."

Laar says reluctantly , "I hope I don't have to do that again."

Ruther agrees, "I hope you don't too. See ya."

***

The dealer asks, "What can I do for you?"

Ruther replies, "I want to buy one thousand tons of assorted dehydrated meats, fruits, and vegetables."

The dealer asks, "When do you need it?"

Ruther answers, "I'm ready to take it now."

The dealer responds, "You must be joking."

Ruther answers, "No. My ship is ready to load as soon as you can deliver."

The dealer continues, "Maybe you haven't heard, but the Cotalion traders bought out our stores completely. Production is being sold on a first come first serve, notes in hand basis. The production is sold up for six weeks already and it could be sold even further ahead. My last information is based on sales up to one hour ago. A big buy could have gone through since then."

Ruther states, "But all I need is one thousand tons. That's a small amount. You must be able to get your hands on that."

The dealer replies, "Well, there are some illegal sales being made by speculators, but the price is very high."

Ruther asks, "How high?"

The dealer says, "One thousand tons should cost you about four hundred thousand notes."

Ruther says, surprised, "What? This stuff was sellin' for fifty notes per ton for fruits, thirty-five for vegetables, and one hundred for meats the last time I bought."

The dealer inquires, "Where did you buy and how long ago? Was it on one of the inner planets?"

Ruther replies, "Yes. About three months ago."

The dealer states, "Maybe you can still get it for that price in the inner sectors, but since Cotalion has entered into the trade picture, prices have gone up to one hundred fifty for fruits, one hundred twenty-five for vegetables, and three hundred for meats on the open market in the sectors bordering on Cotalion. The minerals, metals, and jewels that Cotalion trades with are worth a lot of notes and combined with the inflated demand, they have driven up prices fast."

Ruther advises, "All I have is fifty thousand notes."

The dealer answers, "You can only get about one hundred sixty tons with that. If you go to the speculators, you'll get even less than that."

Ruther says angrily, "Forget it."

The dealer shrugs, "Sorry stranger."

***

Laar inquires, "How did you do, Ruther?"

Ruther answers, "Not so well. Prices have gone wild, and the wait is six weeks for delivery."

Laar interjects, "So, the lander was right."

Ruther asks, "Are we fueled up?"

Laar replies, "All set."

Ruther says disgustedly, "Let's get clearance and leave. We'll head for one of the inner processing planets. The prices there as not as badly inflated."

Laar says, "I'll call Landing Control. *Ibex* to Landing Control. Request clearance for takeoff."

Landing Control inquires, "What is your destination?"

Laar answers, "Just give us a course toward the inner sectors."

Landing Control again inquires, "Don't you have a destination?"

Laar replies, "Not at this time."

Landing Control responds, "You're clear on vector SE27."

Laar replies, "Thanks. *Ibex* out. We're clear, Ruther."

Ruther grumbles, "Let's get out of here."

Laar states, "We had better decide on a destination. We'll be leaving the atmosphere in three hours.

Ruther declares, "This is really goin' to set us back. Let's head for Sector I45. We should be able to get what we need there.

Laar advises, "The planet Nobil is the first processing planet that we'll reach in I45 from here."

Ruther grumbles, "Fine. Head for Nobil. How long will it take us?"

Laar says, "At cruising speed, it will take 36 l-days."

Ruther grumbles, "Isn't there any place closer?"

Laar informs him, "Only in the border sectors."

Ruther says agitated, "Forget it. Head for Nobil. Damn it!"

Chapter 4

Teena

Doctor Deemer orders, "I need a companion sent to my room."

The Companion Master asks, "Who is this?"

"It's Doctor Deemer."

The Companion Master says, annoyed, "You again, Deemer?"

Doctor Deemer commands, "Don't ever call me Deemer again! I am Doctor Deemer. I am not your contemporary. I demand the respect due my position. My privileges are now unlimited since I furnished The Realm with the ultimate weapon. I have been elevated to head scientist of the Defense Section."

The Companion Master replies patronizingly, "I know, Doctor. You tell me that every time you call."

Doctor Deemer yells, "That is because you are an idiot who must be reminded of things over and over. Now send me the companion and make her young. Teens or early twenties. Do you understand?"

The Companion Master answers, "At once. Dispatcher! Send Teena to Deemer's room."

The dispatcher cries, "Not Teena, sir!"

The Companion Master reiterates, "I said Teena!"

The dispatcher argues, "But you know what Deemer did to the last girls we sent to him."

The Companion Master replies, "I know but there are no other girls in his age specifications available. Four of the girls are in the infirmary and the others are being used."

The dispatcher continues to argue. "But Deemer has become brutal now that his privileges are unlimited. There are at least three other girls available to send instead of Teena."

The Companion Master replies, "He had those girls before. If he didn't request them, I can only assume that he wasn't pleased enough to ask for them again. I'm afraid that Deemer might permanently injure them if he gets them a second time."

The dispatcher continues to argue, "But you can't send Teena. She's the sweetest girl that we have. I don't want to see her harmed."

The Companion Master suggests, "Maybe if he gets someone that he likes, he won't torture her. I am hoping that Teena can soften his heart and prevent anyone else from being hurt. Send her now!"

***

Teena introduces herself. "Doctor Deemer, my name is Teena. I was sent for you from the Companion Pool."

Doctor Deemer says lustily, "Such a splendid girl. Why have you never been sent to me before? You are the prettiest that I have ever seen. Drop your clothing, Teena and mix me a cocktail. The bar is over there. Magnificent! Now, Teena, on your knees before your god. Do you realize who you are with? I am Doctor Deemer, the man who created the ultimate weapon for The Realm. My weapon destroys solar systems. It is capable of destroying the entire universe. Do you know what dead solar systems are? Do you know what it takes to destroy a sun? I have the power to destroy the universe at my command. Doesn't that make me a god, Teena? Beg your god for mercy. Do you want to hear how my weapon works? The weapon draws all the energy of the object that it enters inward toward its center creating a reaction that changes the composition of the object's interior without altering its mass or surface appearance. The object is destroyed by its own energy. No outer energy source is needed, making it impossible to detect the cause of the destruction. It appears as though the object simply burns out. Brilliant isn't it, Teena? Plead for your life. Convince me that you are worthy to live. Show me that you are worthy of my attention. If you please me, I may spare you. Worship me!"

***

"Sir, this is the dispatcher. Teena just returned from Deemer. You'd better get down here fast."

The Companion Master inquires, "What happened?"

The dispatcher replies, "Deemer tortured her. I don't know how she made it back."

The Companion Master replies urgently, "I'll be right there. Call the infirmary and have them prepare a room for her."

The dispatcher says consolingly, "Teena, the Master is on his way. He'll take care of you. Just relax. I wish that I could get close enough to Deemer. I would kill him."

The Companion Master says reassuringly, "I'm here, Teena. I am truly sorry for what happened. We are going to the infirmary. Are you able to walk or should I send for a robot to aid you?"

Teena replies, "I'll walk, Master."

The Companion Master asks in astonishment, "What did he do to you?"

Teena replies hysterically, "He is insane. He kept calling himself a god. He made me plead for my life as he tortured me. He is an animal. You can't send him any more girls. He'll torture them like he tortured me. He may even kill one of them. He is a cruel monster. He derives pleasure from the pain and suffering of others."

The Companion Master says soothingly, "Calm down, Teena. Rest. We'll have you back to your beautiful self in no time. Just relax. Orderly, give this girl whatever she asks for and charge it to the Companion Pool. I'll visit you soon, Teena."

Teena replies calmly, "Goodbye, Master."

***

"Sir, this is the dispatcher. Deemer has called and requested Teena. I told him that she is in the infirmary."

The Companion Master inquires, "Who did you send to him?"

The dispatcher replies, "He didn't want anyone except Teena. He wants to be notified as soon as she is out of the infirmary and back on call. It looks like she pleased him. We can't send her back to him, Master. It would be inhuman to make her go through that torture again."

The Companion Master answers reassuringly, "Don't worry. He will never see Teena again. I will see to that personally. I am on my way to see her now."

***

The Companion Master arrives. "Hello, Teena."

Teena replies energetically, "Master. It is nice to see you. I feel well enough to report for work."

The Companion Master answers regretfully, "Teena, Deemer has requested you as soon as you are on call again."

Teena cries, "No, Master! You can't! I am ill! I am not fit to return. Please leave me here. He will torture me again. Have mercy on me, Master. I can't go through that again."

The Companion Master replies reassuringly, "Calm down, Teena. I won't let him have you. But he has requested you and we cannot keep you here forever. Listen to me. I have a plan, but it will require you to leave this planet. I will send you somewhere else where you can work. Are you willing?"

Teena agrees desperately, "Yes! Anything!"

The Companion Master speaks seriously. "Then hear my plan. If I tell Deemer that you are dead, I may be able to get you off the planet. Deemer will naturally think that he is responsible. He can't let that leak out. I will tell him that I will cover up the incident for him by falsifying your sale to one of the vacation planets. But the sale will not be false, I will arrange for you to work on Lexicon. I know the certifier there. I have already explained the circumstances to him, and he has agreed to act as buyer. He will send a ship for you. Once you reach Lexicon, he will certify you and allow you to work there. However, the ship will not arrive for three months. Until it arrives, I will keep you at my residence. You must not be seen by anyone. Once you reach my residence, you will not be allowed to leave the room that I provide until the ship arrives. I will attend to your needs personally until then. Remember, no one will be permitted to see you. You will be lonely but alive."

Teena replies gratefully, "Thank you, Master. I will repay you every night."

The Companion Master counters, "I don't require repayment. On the contrary, I owe you for sending you to that monster in the first place. If anyone has a debt to repay, it is me. Now you just stay put. By tonight, you will be safely at my residence."

***

"Dispatcher, this is the Master. Has Deemer called again?"

The dispatcher replies, "Not yet, sir."

The Companion Master orders, "When he does, put me on with him."

The dispatcher alerts him. "Sir, it's Deemer."

The Companion Master asks, "Does he want Teena?"

The dispatcher answers, "Yes."

The Companion Master orders, "Put me on with him."

The dispatcher informs him, "Doctor Deemer, the Master wishes to speak with you."

Doctor Deemer asks, "What does he want?"

The dispatcher says, "Hold on and I'll connect you."

The Companion Master speaks sternly. "Doctor Deemer, I am the Companion Master."

Doctor Deemer asks, "What do you want?"

The Companion Master continues, "I must speak with you in a private place. It is urgent."

Doctor Deemer, annoyed, says, "I have no time for you. Send me Teena."

The Companion Master states, "She is the reason that we must speak."

Doctor Deemer answers defensively, "You cannot dictate what I do with the companions that you send to me."

The Companion Master states seriously, "I have no intention of dictating anything, but we still must meet."

Doctor Deemer relents. "Very well. Come to the lab and have the guard summon me when you arrive. I will have you sent to the study. We can talk there."

Doctor Deemer snaps, "Guard, I am expecting a visitor from the Companion Pool. Have him escorted to the study and summon me when he arrives."

The Companion Master arrives. "I am here to see Doctor Deemer. I am expected."

The guard inquires, "Who shall I tell him is here?"

The Companion Master answers, "I am from the Companion Pool."

The guard says, "Please follow me."

"Doctor Deemer, the man from the Companion Pool is in the study."

The Companion Master asks, "Doctor Deemer?"

Doctor Deemer sneers, "You must be the Companion Master."

The Companion Master answers, "Yes. Are we alone?"

Doctor Deemer replies, "Yes. You can speak freely here."

The Companion Master states solemnly, "Teena has died."

Doctor Deemer replies defensively, "Why is this my concern? Are you accusing me? I will see to it that you disappear. I am very powerful you know."

The Companion Master states, "I know, Doctor. That is why I want to help you. I wish to stay in your good graces."

Doctor Deemer snaps, "I don't need any help. You are the one who needs the help."

The Companion Master continues, "I can fix it so that no one knows that the girl is dead."

Deemer bellows, "I don't care if she is reported dead."

The Companion Master states, "There will be an investigation. If she isn't reported as dead, there won't be an investigation."

Doctor Deemer asks suspiciously, "I see. And what do you want in return?"

The Companion Master replies, "Just a commendation. I like my post and a good word from you to the administration will carry a lot of weight."

Doctor Deemer inquires, "Are you in some sort of trouble?"

The Companion Master replies, "No. But I have heard rumors that there is an official seeking a master's post when he retires. I don't want him to get mine."

Doctor Deemer, interested, inquires, "Just how will you fix it?"

The Companion Master answers quietly, "I will falsify her sale to one of the vacation planets."

Doctor Deemer snaps, "Which one?"

The Companion Master continues, "I haven't arranged it yet, but it must remain anonymous when I do."

Doctor Deemer growls angrily, "Why should I go along with this? I have nothing to fear. No penalty will be dealt to the man who invented the ultimate weapon. I am too valuable to The Realm. The girl was just a companion."

The Companion Master counters, "But companions are protected by law. Why chance a scandal? You know that it is to your advantage to keep your name clean. Some people have tried to discredit high Realm officials in order to embarrass the Director. I am sure that the Director can handle such things, but why cause him the trouble? He is very busy and prefers that his officials handle their own affairs. Besides, it will cost you no more than a letter."

Doctor Deemer continues angrily, "I have no fear of an investigation. No one would dare accuse me. But if an investigation can be avoided so easily, I will go along with your plan. I don't have any time to spare on investigators. No one can get anything done with those pests snooping around. Do what you must, and you shall have your commendation."

The Companion Master ends, "It was a pleasure talking to you, Doctor."

Doctor Deemer turns his back, "Good day, sir. I will have you escorted out."

Chapter 5

The Venture Fails

Laar states, "There's Nobil. We'll be there in an l-day."

Ruther grumbles, "It's about time. How many notes do we have left to buy with?"

Laar replies, "Well, we should refuel."

Ruther snaps, "We just refueled on Ura."

Laar replies, "You know as well as I that it takes a quarter of our supply to get out of an atmosphere as dense as Ura's."

Ruther states, "That leaves us three quarters full."

Laar counters, "Not after we land on Nobil and take off with a full load. We'd be lucky if we were able to land again on what we'd have left."

Ruther asks annoyed, "All right, so how many will be left after we refuel?"

Laar says, "About forty thousand notes."

Ruther says, "We'll just buy less meat than originally planned. Let's check our gear. That planet is so damned hot that I don't understand how anyone can live there."

Laar states, "It's perfect for dry food processing. They can store the stuff without any special apparatus to keep out moisture."

Ruther agrees. "That's because the planet doesn't have any moisture."

Laar says, "My gear is all in order."

Ruther states, "Mine is all right except for my air shoes. I'll get them fixed after we land, but in the meantime, it looks like I am wearing boots."

Laar warns, "You won't be spending much time on the surface wearing boots."

Ruther replies, "Don't worry about me. I've been subjected to worse."

Laar says, "And you complained like a child."

Ruther changes the subject. "Are we nearin' the atmosphere yet?"

Laar replies, "Almost. I'll call for a vector once we enter." Laar adds, "Bad news. The Fleet has a convoy down there. We're being landed in the middle of nowhere."

Ruther grumbles, "Is anythin' else goin' to go wrong? Just what we needed, another delay."

Laar states, "It's a small planet with good transportation."

Ruther continues, "But it's damn uncomfortable down there."

Laar quips, "Get your shoes fixed and you'll be fine."

Ruther says obstinately, "I'm not leavin' this ship until they're fixed. You'll have to take them to a repair shop for me. I know there won't be any near the port where we land."

Laar replies, "All right, but you'll have to make the preparation for taking the food on board."

Ruther quips, "I'll take care of it."

Laar states, "We'll be down soon."

Ruther says, "Wake me up when we land."

***

Laar returns, "Here are your shoes Ruther."

Ruther asks, "How much did it cost?"

Laar answers, "Five notes. He relined them for you."

Ruther counters,' "All I wanted you to do is have them put back into workin condition again. I don't intend to use them much after we leave Nobil."

Laar argues, "We may be coming back regularly. If our trade goes well, you'll need them."

Ruther replies, "They feel good. It was worth it."

Laar says sarcastically, "Well, how about paying me back then."

Ruther snaps, "Here. Now don't bother me. I'm goin' out to deal."

Laar inquires, "Did you prepare the storage areas?"

Ruther answers, "Yes."

Laar asks, "How about refueling?"

Ruther answers, "Done."

Laar says, "Then I can come with you. There's no need for me to stay behind."

Ruther snaps, "Get your gear on. We don't have all day."

Laar replies, "I'm ready. Let's go."

Ruther asks, "How long will it take us to get to the brokerage area?"

Laar replies, "Near ten hours."

Ruther asks annoyed, "What? Where in the universe did they land us?"

Laar informs, "We're on the other side of the desert."

Ruther asks, "Isn't there any air transportation from here?"

Laar answers, "Sure, but it'll cost us at least twelve notes each to go where we want to go."

Ruther grumbles, "Forget it. We'll take the tube system. That's another day wasted."

Laar states, "It doesn't make any difference. We aren't on a set schedule. No one is waiting for us."

Ruther informs him, "I just want to make some notes so I can get back to Lexicon. Somebody is waitin' for me there."

Laar says sarcastically, "I should have known."

Ruther says, "Well, we made it. I'm exhausted from that trip. I'm in no mood for dealin'."

Laar questions, "I thought you wanted to get back to Lexicon?"

Ruther exclaims, "Let's get dealin'."

Laar adds, "I knew that would change your mood."

Ruther inquires, "What are the rates for dehydrated fruits, vegetables, and meats?"

The dealer answers, "Meats are at one hundred fifty notes per ton, fruits are sixty, and vegetables are fifty.

Ruther states, "The price is up since the last time I was here."

The dealer replies, "Those are the prices that the Fleet is paying."

Ruther growls, "I hate the Fleet."

The dealer says, "Don't say that too loud. Fleet traders are all around here."

Ruther says defiantly, "I don't care. Let me have three hundred tons of vegetables, one hundred fifty of fruits, and one hundred of meats."

The dealer states, "That will cost thirty-nine thousand notes."

Ruther snaps, "I know what it costs. Have it delivered to 119."

The dealer hesitates. "All the way out there?"

Ruther answers, "The Fleet gets all the good ports. When can we have delivery?"

The dealer informs him, "In two days."

Ruther asks, "Can't you deliver any faster?"

The dealer replies, "Not out there."

Ruther relents. "All right. Here's the notes."

The dealer says, "Sign. Come back again. It's a pleasure dealing with you."

Ruther says, "Laar, let's get a couple drinks."

Laar answers, "All I have on me is the five notes that you gave me."

Ruther says, "That's plenty. Let's go."

Laar asks, "Do you know any places here?"

Ruther says emphatically, "Are you kiddin'. I never stop here if I can help it. I think I was here once before, and I swore that I'd never come back. Over there. That place looks good."

Laar jests, "You just like the looks of the sign."

Ruther counters, "Well, if you don't have anythin' else to go by... Hey! This place is nice. Let's grab a table. I can use some food."

Laar asks, "Are you buying?"

Ruther says, "Sure, I'll buy."

The waitress greets them, "Can I help you?"

Ruther replies, "You sure can. Do you have a booth?"

The waitress says, "I only wait on tables."

Ruther flirts, "How about after hours? Can I meet you later?"

The waitress replies, "No. I live with someone."

Ruther backs off. "Too bad. You're a beauty. What's the house specialty?"

The waitress informs them, "Taurian rabbit."

Ruther replies, "I'll take some. How about you Laar?"

Laar says, "I'll try it, and an ale."

The waitress asks, "Domestic or trade stock?"

Laar asks, "Do you have any from 16 Sector?"

The waitress answers, "Yes."

Laar answers, "I'll have that."

Ruther says, "I want a Kyne fizz."

The waitress takes the order. "All right, men."

Laar jabs, "Don't you ever let a girl walk past you without trying to bed her?"

Ruther replies, "Not if she's cute."

Laar adds, "You would have spent your last note on that girl."

Ruther answers, "No. I was hopin' for a date. A little romance."

Laar counters, "Not your style, Ruther."

Ruther counters, "That shows you what you know. I prefer dates to companions any time."

Laar answers sarcastically, "You had me fooled."

Ruther says, "Just drink your ale and enjoy the music."

Laar indicates, "Here come a bunch of Fleeties. Now don't cause any trouble. We'll eat and leave."

Ruther asks, "What's your hurry?"

Laar answers, "I know you when you see Fleeties. There are over a dozen of them who just walked in. Who knows how many more are in the other room."

Ruther snaps, "So what."

Laar says, "I don't feel like being carried out tonight."

Ruther says defiantly, "We can handle any Fleet rat."

Laar replies, "There are too many of them."

Ruther insists, "I'll be calm. They just act like they own a place when they're in a group."

Laar changes the subject, "Good. Here comes the food. The cook couldn't have timed it better. This rabbit is delicious."

Ruther says, "It's all right. Hey, sweets, another fizz. Do you want another ale?"

Laar declines. "No. I'm fine."

Ruther points. "Look at those creeps."

Laar asks, "Are you done eating?"

Ruther grumbles, "I'm not finished with my drink."

Laar says emphatically, "Well, finish and let's go."

Ruther relents. "All right, I'm getting' tired of the atmosphere in here anyway."

Laar says, "Let's get back to the *Ibex*. I'm staying aboard the ship tomorrow. How about you, Ruther?"

Ruther replies, "I guess so. It's even hot at night here. I can't wait to leave this planet. How long do you think it'll take us to get out of Stasia and into Cotalion?"

Laar informs him, "It should take us about forty-six l-days if we don't have to dodge any border patrols along the way."

Ruther complains, "Damn space travel takes forever in this cargo vessel of ours. I always wanted to buy an old battle cruiser and convert it. They can really move."

Laar ignores him. "There's the port. Let's get some sleep."

Ruther interjects, "We have all day tomorrow to sleep. Let's down a bottle of haze."

Laar says, "Down it by yourself."

Ruther rails, "All right, creep. I will. I'll tune in on some good music and relax. Maybe I'll get myself an android to keep me company next trip. After we return from Cotalion, I'll be able to afford one."

Laar ignores him. "Goodnight, Ruther."

***

Laar informs him, "This is it, Ruther. We're only 11-hour from the border."

Ruther inquires, "Any patrols in the area?"

Laar answers, "I haven't picked up on any. There are no planets within an l-day of here so we should be clear of scanner stations."

Ruther adds, "Once we're across, they won't follow us even if they do spot us."

Laar exclaims, "Here we go. Fifteen l-minutes and we'll be across. Now all we have to worry about is the type of reception we get from Cotalion. Wait! We're slowing down. We're at dead stop!"

Ruther bellows, "That's impossible!"

Laar reiterates, "We're stopped and that's a fact."

Ruther is puzzled. "Now what do we do?"

Laar states, "We wait for the patrol to reach us."

Ruther is annoyed. "Patrol. I thought you said there were no patrols in the area."

Laar answers, "I just picked it up on the scanner. Three fighters. They'll be here in twenty l-minutes."

Ruther ponders, "I wonder what they'll do to us."

Laar reminds, "You know as well as I that no vessel is permitted to go from Stasia across the galactic border."

Ruther gestures. "We didn't cross."

Laar says, "We tried."

Ruther asks, "What's the penalty?"

Laar responds, "I'm not sure. It happens so rarely that it isn't even listed in most books."

Ruther interjects, "Well, it looks like we're goin' to find out."

"This is Realm Border Patrol Task Group 2 from Passel. Prepare to be boarded. Remain unarmed or we will open fire at the sight of a weapon. Identify yourself.

Laar responds, "This is the independent transport *Ibex*."

The Border Patrol officer demands, "How many are aboard? Identify each person."

"I am Laar of Crellian and my shipmate is Ruther of Kyne. There is no one else aboard.

The Border Patrol officer continues, "What is your cargo?"

Laar replies, "Food. The dehydrated variety."

The Border Patrol officer responds, "Your registration checks out. You will now be boarded. Open your hatch lock, sit in your seats, and don't move. What was your purpose? Your course would have taken you into Cotalion."

Laar makes an excuse. "We were out of control."

The Border Patrol officer informs him, "I will test your ship's systems for signs of failure."

Ruther adds, "We just got back under control when we stopped dead. Somethin' had to be wrong for us to stop dead."

The Border Patrol officer informs him, "You were caught in a magno-net."

Ruther grunts, "What in stars is that?"

The Border Patrol officer answers, "It is a high power, extreme range magnetic field charged with a power damper. A border trap."

Ruther asks, "Do you have these across the entire border?"

The Border Patrol officer answers, "Only where our scanner stations are out of range. You will be escorted to the holding ports on Passel."

Ruther wonders, "Then what?"

The Border Patrol officer replies, "Then you will be questioned by the authorities. Follow my ship and do not veer from course or—"

Ruther snaps, "I know. Or we will be blasted out of space. Let's eat somethin', Laar. I want to have a full stomach when we face the authorities."

***

The authorities state, "Laar of Orellion and Ruther of Kyne, there is no question to the fact that you were attempting to cross the Stasia/Cotalion Border. This is forbidden by the laws of The Realm. The purpose of the law which you violated is to prevent an inter-galactic incident. Your vessel will be confiscated and the cargo turned over to a licensed broker for immediate sale."

Ruther protests, "Wait a—"

The authorities interrupt, "Be silent! You have nothing to say. It is done. We don't want your kind on this planet. We will transport you to whichever planet you choose by whatever method we have at our disposal. Where do you wish to be sent?"

Ruther answers, "I want to go to Lexicon."

Laar blurts, "Ruther, are you crazy?"

Ruther answers, "We can get work there."

Laar questions, "Doing what?"

Ruther answers, "Tendin' bar or somethin'. Where else can we go and find immediate work? And don't tell me on a minin' or factory planet."

Laar says, "All right. I will go to Lexicon too."

The authorities advise, "You may return to your vessel to remove your gear and personal belongings. Then you will return to this station to be held in detention until your transportation is arranged. If you fail to return, I will have you killed on sight as fugitives."

Ruther responds, "Yes, sir."

***

Ruther mutters, "This is the bottom of the barrel. Bein' locked in a storage hold with android parts is bad enough. But to be locked up on a Fleet vessel, I'll never be able to live it down. They have us sealed up in here with no light and when the door opens, the first thing we'll see is a wise guy fleet rat. And we'll have to take his abuse or we won't get fed. Then they'll feed us some lousy leftovers. I'll remember their faces and the next time I see them, I'll get even."

Laar interjects, "At least this way we're going to reach Lexicon without it costing us anything. I think free transportation is worth any abuse we receive. Do you have any idea where we are going to get a job once we reach Lexicon?"

Ruther answers, "I know bar owners and inn keepers all over the planet. We won't have any trouble. But they won't pay much. How many notes do we have left?"

Laar answers, "We have one thousand left from the notes we used to buy the food. Another eight thousand that I set aside for fuel. And another two hundred ten of my own."

Ruther says, "Add twenty-six notes to that and we have nine thousand two hundred thirty-six."

Laar questions, "Twenty-six notes. Is that all you have left?"

Ruther reminds him, "Don't forget, dinner was on me on Nobil."

Laar counters, "That cost you sixteen notes. You went through a bundle on Lexicon."

Ruther snaps, "Now I'll make it back on Lexicon."

Laar fires back, "And you'll spend every note that you earn."

Laar states, "We'll have to get a room when we get there. That'll cost about five hundred notes a month. Then we'll need to save up enough to buy a small craft to get us back to Passel. We'll need to have some notes to try to buy back the *Ibex* too."

Ruther answers, "It would be a lot cheaper to book fare aboard a passenger vessel than it would to buy a craft. Better yet, we can sign aboard a freighter and work our way to Passel."

Laar replies, "That sounds fine except you can't sign on a freighter for only one way."

Ruther replies, "So, we'll pay off the captain to get replacements for us for the return trip. Captains never turn down the chance to make a few extra notes, especially since findin' replacements is usually easy. Then if we can't get the *Ibex* back, we have the return trip to Lexicon already arranged."

Laar agrees, "I guess that will work out. I just hope they give us the *Ibex* back. That commandant didn't look like the type that takes bribes. And by the time we get back to Passel, he will probably have turned the *Ibex* over to the Fleet."

Ruther notes, "The tough ones can fool you. He'll probably keep it around for a while just to see if we return for it."

Laar sighs. "Well, there's no sense in worrying about it until the time comes."

Ruther gestures. "Right. The first thing that I'm goin' to do when I get to Lexicon is visit my girls."

Laar interrupts him. "Now wait a minute. We need all of the notes that we have. You wait until you earn enough to pay for them out of your own pocket."

Ruther replies, "I'll borrow it and pay it back."

Laar warns, "You'd better watch your spending because I'm going to make you pay back every note."

Ruther gestures. "I tell you what I'll do. I'll introduce you to them. That way you can have some fun too."

Laar objects. "No thanks. We won't be able to afford to pay for both of us."

Ruther continues, "These girls love me. They'll let you come along as long as you are with me. They won't charge extra. I take care of them and they take care of me."

Laar quips, "So that's where all your notes go."

Ruther replies, "They're well worth it. They're the best. I never found anyone else who could even come close."

Laar says sarcastically, "What happens when you can't support them anymore?"

Ruther says vehemently, "I'll support them. No matter what happens, I'll support them."

Laar asks sarcastically, "If we're going to support them, why don't we move in with them?"

Ruther blurts back, "You creep. Forget it. And we aren't goin' to support them. I am."

Laar backs off. "Don't get so upset. You really care about these girls, don't you."

Ruther emphasizes, "You bet I do. And they aren't goin' to find out that we lost the *Ibex* either. Understand!"

Laar answers, "Whatever you say."

***

Ruther says, "It seemed like we would never get here. Let's head for the Oxline Inn. We'll get a room and clean up. Then we'll see about getting some work."

Laar asks, "Is there any reason why you chose the Oxline?"

Ruther replies, "Nice rooms and near the action."

Laar states, "This whole planet is full of action. I don't know how you could be away from the action anywhere on this planet. But for lack of a better suggestion, let's go."

Ruther says, "I'm goin' for a bartender's job at the Lustar. Why don't you come with me?"

Laar states, "I can't bartend."

Ruther says, "So, try for a cook's job. If there's one thing you're good at, its cookin'."

Laar concurs. "Not a bad idea. I'll try."

Ruther indicates, "Here it is. It's a pretty nice place, isn't it."

Laar agrees, "Looks all right to me."

Ruther yells, "Hey, Jimmi!"

Jimmi is surprised, "Ruther! You're back again. Just can't stay away from Lexicon can you."

Ruther asks, "Is Hack around?"

Jimmi replies, "He's in the office. Do you want me to tell him you're here?"

Ruther answers, "Tell him I want to talk to him."

Jimmi jests, "Oh stars! What are you selling now."

Ruther replies, "Not this time. Me and my partner Laar ran into some difficulty on Passel. I want to see if we can get some work."

Jimmi inquires, "What happened? Did you crash the *Ibex*?"

Ruther answers, "No. It was confiscated."

Jimmi asks, "You weren't selling restricted cargo, were you?"

Ruther blurts, "Will you stop the questions and tell Hack that I'm here."

Jimmi yells, "Hack! Are you busy?"

Hack asks, "Why?"

Jimmi answers, "Ruther is out here. He wants to talk to you."

Hack asks sarcastically, "What is he selling now?"

Jimmi answers, "Nothing. He just wants to talk."

Hack responds, "Well, send him in and bring us a round of ale."

Jimmi gestures, "Go ahead in, Ruther. And good luck."

Ruther gestures, "Come on, Laar."

Hack is cordial. "Ruther, how are you?"

Ruther mutters, "To tell you the truth, I'm not so good."

Hack is surprised. "Oh?"

Ruther points, "This is my partner Laar."

Hack is cordial. "Glad to meet you. What do you mean, not so good? That isn't like you."

Ruther is downhearted. "The *Ibex* was confiscated. Can you give us jobs?"

Hack asks, "How in stars did you manage that?"

Ruther is nonchalant. "It just happened."

Hack says sarcastically, "I'll bet they picked you up for nothing at all."

Ruther quips, "How about the jobs, Hack?"

Hack asks, "What can you do?"

Ruther answers, "I can tend bar and Laar can cook."

Hack inquires, "Cook? Are you any good? I could always use another cook. You could relieve some of the load in the kitchen."

Laar is enthusiastic. "I'm a great cook."

Hack is all business. "I'll pay you seventeen notes a day plus meals while you're on. As far as you go, Ruther, I'll give you eight notes a night plus meals. You'll do all right on tips. Is it a deal?"

Ruther agrees. "Deal."

Hack inquires, "What hotel are you staying at?"

Ruther answers, "The Oxline."

Hack asks, "How much are you paying?"

Ruther replies, "Five hundred a month."

Hack states, "At that rate you'll be working just to pay for your room. If you go for one of the smaller rooms, I can get you a deal as one of my employees. I can get you a room for two hundred."

Ruther accepts, "Sounds good. We'll take it. When do we start?"

Hack asks, "How about tomorrow?"

Ruther counters, "How about the day after?"

Hack gives in. "All right. I know what you're up to."

Laar says, "I'll start tomorrow."

Hack is pleased. "Good. You're the one I really need. I'll see you tomorrow at seven o'clock."

Laar is excited. "How about that, Ruther. With the deal he's getting us on the room, we'll be able to save a good amount each month toward the *Ibex*."

Ruther replies, "It pays to have friends. But don't expect the room to be much."

Laar continues, "I don't care. I'm looking forward to saving enough notes to leave here and recover the Ibex. If I intended to settle here, it might make a difference."

Ruther, relieved says, "Well, now that we're all set, I'm goin' to see my girls. Do you want to come along?"

Laar declines. "No. I think that I'll stay and rest. I'm starting work tomorrow."

Ruther says, "I'll see you in a couple of days."

Chapter 6

Cotalion

"This is Brodis, Chief of Intelligence. Connect me with the Director.

The attendant responds, "Yes, sir. Director, Brodis is on the viewer for you."

The Director answers, "I have it attendant. Brodis, have you come up with a plan?"

Brodis replies, "No, sir. But I have a report for you. We have lost a few reconnaissance craft but I was able to gather some new data. Cotalion has chosen to agriculturalize a group of systems on the far side of their galaxy. The chosen sites will not be easily accessible from Stasia. From the information that I have, their efforts have barely begun. I am not sure of the information that was contained in the lost ships, so my information is piecemeal. If we are to disrupt their operations, we must penetrate clear through Cotalion or attempt to travel outside of the galaxy in open space in an effort to circle around to the far border of Cotalion. The latter would take considerably longer but would stand a far greater chance for success."

The Director says, "Do what you must but do not allow yourself to be detected. The operation is in your hands. Just remember that The Realm cannot be implicated in any way."

Brodis affirms, "Yes, sir. Signing off."

***

The Council Speaker announces, "This emergency session of the High Council of Cotalion is now in order. The First Councilman is presiding."

The First Councilman is speaking. "We have thus far been unable to determine the cause of the deadening of our prime agricultural solar systems. We have attributed it to natural causes but my scientific knowledge leads me to believe otherwise. I don't believe that it is possible for a sun to die out without first going through several stages of degeneration. I therefore must call for a continuation of the present investigation. I have studied all of the data which each member of this council has compiled. Very little progress has been made regarding the agriculturalization of other solar systems to replace the ones that were lost. Councilman, this project is your responsibility. If I don't see some progress soon, I will move to have you relieved of your responsibility.

"We are still buying food from Stasia, but so far Stasia's officials have ignored all of our attempts to contact them. They have not responded to any of our transmissions, but they aren't offering any resistance or protest to our ships entering Stasia and trading with their planets either. Two possibilities occur to me. Either Stasia is a galaxy comprised of independent planets, which is unlikely, or their governing body has not decided how to handle the situation that we have created for them. As long as we are able to obtain enough food from them, we will continue as we have, trading with the closest planets to our border. In that manner we will be able to send assistance if our cargo ships are attacked. We will keep our border patrols on constant alert and have our battle cruisers on standby. I doubt the integrity of any authority that refuses to acknowledge the transmissions of another government. I want an end to this trade as soon as possible. It has become far too costly. For the first time, our wealth is being poured into another galaxy. It is not a healthy situation."

The councilman replies, "We have been unable to contact any planet in the Septis Galaxy. Worse yet, any ship that has been sent to Septis, has not been heard from again. I have fortified our sectors bordering Septis to the best of our capability but Septis is much larger than Stasia and I fear the possibility of a conflict. I don't like the fact that they have performed acts of aggression against our ships but so far they have not attempted to invade Cotalion. We must concentrate our efforts on agriculturalization. We cannot afford a war at this time, so we will not retaliate. I am satisfied to keep the status quo. We will not send any more ships to Septis. We can no longer consider Septis as a viable possibility for new trade. Unless we are able to obtain a response from Stasia, our situation is fixed. According to our trading ships, the inhabitants of the planets in Stasia that they have visited are humanoids of the same nature and intelligence as ourselves. They seem to possess a technology at least equal to ours."

The First Councilman responds, "Our traders have been given every courtesy and in fact seem to have been given priority over ships from their own galaxy in many cases. I can't understand their lack of response. Can any of the Council members add anything to my summary? Then I suggest that you all resume your usual duties. Our efficiency in all areas is absolutely essential at this time. If anyone uncovers any new information, they are to report it to me immediately. This Council is in recess until further notice."

The Security Chief calls, "First Councilman."

The First Councilman responds, "What is it?"

The Security Chief states, "You know as well as I that unidentified ships have been sighted in our galaxy. Once they realize that they've been seen, they run to avoid being identified. In fact if they realize that they can't outrun us, they self-destruct. Why didn't you mention this at the meeting?"

The First Councilman replies, "Until I know more about those ships and their mission, I don't want word of their presence to leak out."

The Security Chief speculates, "It seems that we are being spied on."

The First Councilman acknowledges this. "Yes, and I want to know who is behind it. It could be a subversive group from within our galaxy or they could be from Septis. Even more likely, they are from Stasia. Since our ships are entering Stasia regularly, it is reasonable to believe that they are trying to find out more about us."

The Security Chief continues, "But why the secrecy? We have tried to contact them, and they have refused to reply. They could find out more about us easily if they communicated with us."

The First Councilman emphasizes, "Which leads me to believe that they are a devious race who cannot be trusted. Just continue your vigilance. I must know more before I release any news."

Chapter 7

A Pirate is Convicted

The prosecutor speaks. "The Penal Court will now decide the fate of Radam. He was once the leader of The Realm's primary attack force. He is reported to have disappeared after resigning his commission following the news of his being relieved of command and his reassignment to a teaching post at the Academy. After his disappearance, a series of pirate activities began to occur throughout the outer sectors. Radam was later apprehended on planet Vella with a band of pirates. In their possession was a shipload of weapons ranging from lightweight sidearms, to heavy missile launchers, to long range anti-spacecraft cannons. These weapons were found to be the same weapons that were hijacked from the three military freighters that were reported missing in transit from border attack base S2 to the central attack base on Kyne.

"Radam was also identified as the leader of the pirate band that was preventing trade vessels from approaching the planet Talis, thus disrupting the economy of the planet. This act was done in retaliation to a refusal by Talis to sell food to an unregistered vessel. Radam has been convicted of piracy, hijacking, possession of stolen military weapons, murder, and attempting to destroy the economy of a planet."

The judge inquires, "Does the Court have a decision?"

The jury responds, "It is the decision of this court that Radam be condemned to live out life on the ice planet Duron. He will be given one set of protective gear and one last meal before he is abandoned on Duron. The last scan has revealed that there is no humanoid life presently on Duron. We must thereby conclude that all persons previously sentenced to Duron are now dead. Radam will be on his own to survive for as long as he is able. In the meantime, he is to be held on the prison shuttle that will deliver him to Duron."

The judge commands, "Take the prisoner away. Have him fitted with protective gear and find out what he wishes as his last meal."

***

The jailor sneers, "This is it, Radam. It looks nice and cold. I wouldn't wish this on anyone. I hope you enjoyed your meal. It could be a long time before you have another. Have a pleasant stay. Now walk."

Radam replies defiantly, "My chances of survival are slim, but I will live to strike back at The Realm for all they've done to me. Mark my words."

The jailor commands, "Walk!"

***

The planet Duron is an ice planet with some small plant life and a few species of insects and bacteria. There is no animal life at all. Radam would be hard pressed to find food. His first task would be to find suitable shelter because he would not be able to survive in an ice storm even with his protective gear. If his gear was to tear or wear out, he would be unable to repair or replace it. This would mean as certain a death as the starvation that faced him.

The only thing in abundance on Duron is ice. But the ice on Duron is strange. It is made up of many different colors depending on where you look. For instance, a single column of brown ice may stick up in the middle of a flat plain. Or a protrusion of blue ice may cover part of a mountain wall. Certain other formations are yellow, or green, or clear.

No study has ever been made of the planet's terrain. The climate is too severe to support colonization. The ice is too thick to cut through easily, making it too difficult for mining. Farming is out of the question because of the climate. The Realm has no productive use for Duron and has no desire to sink any time or resources into its study. But The Realm finds a use for almost every planet and Duron is no exception. It has become one of the most dreaded planets of exile for criminals in the entire Realm. To be sent to Duron is looked upon as being sent to your execution. But Radam is a survivor, and he won't die without a struggle. He is determined to live through this ordeal if for no other reason than to get revenge on The Realm. He set out to familiarize himself with his environment and to find a shelter.

It didn't take him long to find one. There was an overhang covering a deep crevasse in the ice. He made this his shelter to protect him from the wind and storms. He found certain plants that were edible but they were few and far between and it took a great deal to find them. As he searched for food, he began examining the different types of ice. He found that the clear ice was pure and much harder than the other colors which contained impurities. He was able to make chisels out of the sharply pointed clear icicles. He learned that the yellow ice had a sulfur content. He was able to use plant fiber to filter the sulfur from the ice which he pulverized and melted with his body heat. He used friction and sticks that he treated with sulfur to start fires for warmth. He was also able to fashion torches for light. But food was still scarce. He had to find some way to grow a food supply.

One day he examined one of the lone brown ice columns closely. He discovered that a tree trunk was what gave the column its color. He knew that the tree had to be anchored in the ground, no matter how much ice was around it. He set himself to work with torches and ice chisels and after a few days, he exposed the base of the tree trunk. He set the exposed wood on fire and by burning the tree trunk, exposed a patch of ground where the trunk had been. He fashioned a type of ice shelter over the patch and moved his quarters into the shelter. He then planted some of the seeds, that he got from other plants, into his newly formed garden. They grew like weeds since they were hardy seeds capable of growing in the severe climate of the planet. They thrived in abundance in the protected conditions of his garden, and he now had a more than adequate food supply. He had learned to survive where no one had succeeded before him. Survival was no longer the question. But would he ever be able to escape from the planet? It was off limits to all vessels. No one was permitted to land on Duron, or even to enter its atmosphere without authorization. The planet was sealed off. Radam was isolated.

Chapter 8

A Chance Meeting

Laar says, "I have the night off, Ruther."

Ruther asks, "Did you make plans?"

Laar answers, "I'm going out for dinner. It'll be nice to have someone cook for me for a change."

Ruther asks, "Are you goin' alone?"

Laar answers, "Yes."

Ruther asks, "Why don't you pick up a companion?"

Laar responds, "I don't think so. See you later."

***

Laar requests, "I would like a table for one please."

The host replies, "Sorry. We're pretty busy tonight."

Teena requests, "Table for one please."

The host replies, "I'm sorry but we have no single seats available."

Laar asks, "Miss, would you like to share a table with me?"

Teena replies, "All right. That would solve both of our problems."

Laar requests, "Table for two please."

The host signals, "Right this way."

"My name is Laar."

"I'm Teena. Do you live on Lexicon or are you a transient?"

Laar answers, "I'm a cook at the Lustar."

Teena answers cordially, "Oh. I know Hack pretty well. I'm a companion and I made it a point to know almost all the bar owners and inn keepers for business purposes."

Laar is surprised. "You're a companion? You're beautiful. Why aren't you with anyone? You don't seem like someone who would be lacking for work."

Teena responds, "No. You're right. I'm usually very busy, but I'm in the middle of my cycle, so I will be unable to work for a few days."

Laar asks, "Would you like to see a show with me tonight?"

Teena answers, "Sure."

Laar asks, "What will it cost?"

Teena reiterates, "I told you I'm not working tonight."

Laar is shocked. "You aren't like any other companion I've met before."

Teena states, "Please, I'm not a companion tonight. I am your date."

Laar says happily, "I like that idea."

Teena suggests, "Let's just enjoy the evening together."

***

Ruther inquires, "Hey, Laar, where have you been? I expected you to get home long before me. Did you grab a companion after all?"

Laar answers, "In a manner of speaking. I had dinner with a girl named Teena. She's a companion but she was off tonight. She's the most beautiful girl I've ever met."

Ruther jests, "A companion who isn't busy can't be that great."

Laar states, "She's on her cycle."

Ruther asks, "What did you do all this time? Dinner couldn't last this long."

Laar answers, "We had dinner and went to a show. Then we took a stroll and talked a while. She's fantastic to be with. I asked her out again as a date and she said she'd leave my next day off open."

Ruther says, "This sounds serious."

Laar suggests, "It could be."

Ruther advises, "Well, cool off a while and get some sleep. You have to work tomorrow."

Laar retreats. "Have a nightcap for me, Ruther. Good night."

***

"Hi, Teena. It's Laar."

Teena responds, "Just a minute. I'll let you in."

Laar is stunned. "You look beautiful."

Teena answers, "I wouldn't be seen out like this."

Laar states, "You don't ever need to worry about the way you look."

Teena answers, "I must, Laar. My profession."

Laar assures her, "You're perfect in every way."

Teena blushes. "Oh, Laar. You are very kind. What shall we do today?"

Laar suggests, "After breakfast, I thought we might take the transport to the lake."

Teena answers, "That sounds nice. I enjoy swimming."

Laar is pleased. "Good. It's settled then. What do you like for breakfast? I can prepare pretty near anything."

Teena suggests, "How about an omelet?"

Laar asks, "Any particular type?"

Teena responds, "Make the one you enjoy the most."

Laar says, "All right."

Teena offers, "I'll get some coffee and juice. That smells great. I can't wait to eat."

Laar responds, "You don't have to. It's done."

Teena eats. "Tastes great."

Laar informs her, "I used the mushrooms you had and added some tantle spices."

Teena is enthusiastic. "I love it."

Laar asks, "Can I have some more coffee, Teena?"

Teena pours. "Here you are. Now just relax while I get ready to go. I'll pack a lunch."

Laar offers, "Why don't you let me make the lunch?"

Teena insists, "No. You relax. I want to do it."

Teena affirms, "I'm ready. Let's go, Laar."

Laar compliments her. "How do you do it? Every time I see you, you're more beautiful than before."

Teena prods him. "Let's go, Laar or we'll miss the transport. It should be at the station in a few minutes."

Laar insists, "Let me carry that bag."

Teena yields. "Thank you."

Laar gestures. "Here it comes. Hop on."

The conductor mutters, "Half-note please."

Laar leads the way. "Here you are. Teena, there are two seats over there. Do you want the window? It should only take us about an hour. Do you go there often?"

Teena answers, "No. I usually go to a pool to swim. My customers either take me to dinner or to dance, then straight back to my room. I don't get the chance to go too far. I'm quite busy. You are the first person who I've gone out with more than once non-professionally. I like you. You're different. You're comfortable to be with. That's why I left today open. I enjoy your company. With you, I can relax."

Laar admits, "I like your company too, Teena. I looked forward to today as soon as we parted last. That's why I called you so early. I wanted to spend as much time as possible with you."

Teena is happy. "We'll have a nice day."

***

Laar yells, "Ruther!"

Ruther inquires, "How did it go?"

Laar answers excitedly, "Terrific. We're going to continue to see each other. But we had a chance to talk and get to know one another and we started talking about our families and our past."

Ruther quips, "So?"

Laar continues, "She was a companion on the science research planet where all of The Realm's top researchers are sent. She had a bad experience with one of the scientists there, and she was helped to sneak off the planet. It seems that this cruel scientist was bragging that he was a god and that he created the ultimate weapon for The Realm."

Ruther says sarcastically, "I feel safer already."

Laar continues, "You know those dead systems in Cotalion that you keep wondering about. Well. This nut claims that his weapon caused them."

Ruther says, surprised, "What? That's impossible."

Laar continues, "Apparently, it isn't. Teena said he was bragging about finding a catalyst that could be implanted in a sun to cause the elements in the sun's core to react in such a way as to neutralize each other without changing the mass or appearance of the sun. The sun just goes dead. He said it could not be detected."

Ruther becomes serious. "If that's true, it's serious. The Realm could be preparin' to destroy Cotalion. We don't even know anythin' about Cotalion. I wonder why The Realm wants to destroy it. We have to let someone know what's goin' on."

Laar asks, "But who? There's no one who can oppose The Realm and we have no way of getting to Cotalion to warn them."

Ruther replies, "I know who to tell, but we'll need a ship to get there."

Laar asks, "Who?"

Ruther replies, "Have you ever heard of The Order of the Universe?"

Laar questions, "Do you mean that religious group that lives on Vendra in isolation?"

Ruther replies, "Yes. Do you know what they stand for?"

Laar admits, "Not exactly."

Ruther explains, "They believe in universal balance. They are pledged to protect the Universe against any unsettlin' forces that could disrupt the universal balance. I'm sure they've been tryin' to find out about those dead systems. If they find out they're not natural, they'll do somethin' about it."

Laar is skeptical, "What can they do? They live out there alone. They couldn't possibly challenge the might of The Realm."

Ruther counters, "I wouldn't be so sure. Remember from your history about the Battle of Sector C8 that decided the outcome of the last galactic war? No one knows why the other fleet stopped firin' at The Realm fleet. But they did and they were blown right out of space. Every ship was destroyed. Some people believe that The Order of the Universe was behind the mystery. They pledged to put a stop to the war in order to restore stability to Stasia and prevent any further disruption to the universal balance."

Laar quips, "That's just a story."

Ruther replies, "Maybe. But if anyone can stop The Realm, I believe they can. We must get a craft and go to Vendra."

Laar informs him, "We don't have the notes."

Ruther says, "We'll borrow them if we have to."

Laar hesitates, "But I don't want to leave Teena. I love her."

Ruther is serious. "This is important, Laar. Talk to Teena. She'll wait for you to return if she feels the same way."

Laar reconsiders. "You're really serious about this, aren't you. I've never seen you so concerned about anything before."

Ruther reiterates, "This is important, Laar."

Laar relents, "All right. I'll talk to Teena. You see about a craft."

Ruther adds, "Maybe Teena knows someone who can help us. Ask her."

***

"Teena, it's Laar."

Teena answers, "I'll open up. Hi, I missed you."

Laar replies, "I missed you too, Teena."

Teena asks, "Do you want anything?"

Laar gestures, "Only you, Teena."

Teena blushes. "Oh, Laar."

Laar continues, "Teena, do you remember what you told me about that cruel scientist? Well, I told my roommate Ruther about it because he was always interested in those dead systems in Cotalion. After I told him your story, he became very upset. He says he must relay the story to the Order of the Universe on Vendra. I've been Ruther's partner since I was sixteen. We bought a small cargo ship and went into business as traders four years ago. We have been traveling together ever since. He asked me if I would go with him. I told him I didn't want to leave you but he asked me to explain how important this trip is. Teena, do you know where we can get a craft? I want to go with Ruther. I just can't let him go off alone. This trip is too far. But I can't lose you either. Please wait for me. I love you."

Teena pleads, "Oh, Laar. I love you too. Please let me go along."

Laar replies caringly, "This trip could be dangerous and depending on the type of craft that we get, it could be very uncomfortable."

Teena assures him, "I'm really very durable. I can adapt to almost any situation."

Laar continues, "I'd love to have you with me but you shouldn't have to go through a trip like this."

Teena insists. "Go through what? I want to be with you."

Laar relents. "Let me check with Ruther. I don't think he'd object. I still don't know where we'll get a craft. We don't have near enough notes to buy one."

Teena asks, "Why don't we just book passage to Vendra?"

Laar states, "Vendra is in Sector C8. It's far away and there's nothing near the planet. Only trading vessels go to Vendra regularly, and very few of those."

Teena says, "If we went to the nearest settled planet, we could probably charter a shuttle to Vendra."

Laar answers, "Maybe. Let's talk to Ruther together. He works tonight, so you'll have to come home with me late after he gets off."

Teena inquires romantically, "What do you have planned for today, Laar?"

***

Laar says, "Hi, Ruther."

Ruther asks, "What're you doin' up?"

Laar gestures. "Meet Teena. Teena, this is my partner Ruther."

Ruther says flirtatiously, "You're a winner. Laar wasn't lyin' when he described you."

Laar says, "Take it easy, Ruther. She came back with me to talk about the trip to Vendra. She wants to come with us."

Ruther replies, "She'd be nice company, but this is goin' to be a long hard trip."

Laar says, "I told her that, but she says she's been through this type of thing before and she didn't have any problems."

Ruther gestures, "Hold on. Before we go any farther, I looked around and the least expensive craft available that was suitable for our trip costs two hundred thousand notes. At best we have twenty-five thousand between us. They want one hundred twenty thousand down."

Laar replies, "Teena had mentioned the idea of booking passage to the nearest settled planet to Vendra and then hiring someone to shuttle us to Vendra from there. We could afford that."

Ruther answers, "Maybe, but it would leave us near broke. It will cost us about five thousand notes each to get near enough to Vendra to hire a shuttle. And who knows what a shuttle will cost. It won't be cheap."

Teena informs them, "No. I will pay my own way. I have a large sum saved up. Don't forget, I am one of the most sought after companions on Lexicon. I live expensively, but I am still able to accumulate most of what I earn."

Laar adds, "We will be able to travel comfortably instead of being cramped up in a small craft."

Ruther agrees. "I'm sold. I'll make the arrangements tomorrow."

Laar states, "We have to give Hack notice."

Ruther says, "I'll talk to Hack. Now let's drink to our new travel partner."

Chapter 9

Iceman

"This is Patrol Ship 3 to Patrol Ship Leader. I am registering a considerable disturbance on the planet surface."

Patrol Leader says, "Describe your readings."

Patrol 3 replies, "Large intense flashes of light."

Patrol Leader asks, "Can you speculate on their origin?"

Patrol 3 responds, "My readings don't show any seismic activity. Maybe it's a reflection on the ice."

Patrol Leader orders, "Someone may have slipped past us. Go in and investigate. Keep in constant radio contact."

"Patrol 3 going down for a look."

Radam thinks to himself, *Good. I've attracted a patrol ship. As far as they know I'm dead like all the others exiled here before me. I've learned to slow my life functions almost to the point of suspension. Their instruments would not register humanoid life. My sulfur gas propelled projectiles have attracted attention. Now I must get the patrol ship to fire at that red ice wall at the base of the mountain. The frozen gas will expand once heated and force him down if I can lure him in close enough. I know how to reactivate the ship once I bring it down. The gas will merely stall his engines. Now to open fire with my ice missiles. I hope the range is sufficient to provoke a strafing attack.*

"This is Patrol 3. I am being fired upon by some sort of ground to air missile bombardment. The weapon seems to be very short range. Someone is down there all right. I'm going in."

"This is Patrol Leader. Do you require assistance?"

Patrol 3 replies, "No, Leader. I believe I can handle this alone. If I need help, I'll advise you."

"This is Patrol Leader standing by."

Patrol 3 reports, "It looks like someone built a small ground installation. I get only one life reading. Do you think Radam is still alive?"

Patrol Leader states, "His life readings died over two years ago. No. I think someone has slipped past us."

Patrol 3 inquires, "But why would anyone want to land on Duron? And why don't I pick up any signs of a ship on my instruments?"

Patrol Leader replies, "I don't know but Duron is off limits to all, and if someone is down there, we must apprehend them."

Patrol 3 advises, "I'm close enough to strike but I think I'll make a pass first just to see if I am able to identify anything."

Patrol Leader cautions, "Isn't that a bit careless? You're still being fired upon, aren't you?"

Patrol 3 replies, "Yes, but I can easily outmaneuver this weapon."

Patrol Leader suggests, "He may be trying to lure you in close. I suggest that you strafe him as you make your pass just to protect yourself."

Patrol 3 advises, "Very well. I'm going in now."

Patrol Leader inquires, "What is happening Patrol 3? Come in."

"This is Patrol 3. I fired a maximum angle random barrage, and the installation blew sky high. What an explosion! It seems to have stalled my engines. I'm making a forced landing.

Patrol Leader informs him, "I'm coming down to assist. Send me a homing signal."

Patrol 3 replies, "All right. I'll try to get going again before you arrive."

"This is Patrol Leader to Patrol 2, 4, and 5. I'm going to assist Patrol 3 on the planet surface. Form a triangular cover pattern around the planet and await further orders.

Radam observes, *He's down. It worked. Now I've got him. As soon as he steps out to check his ship, I'll take him. Perfect! I'll open fire with my ice missiles. Got him before he could even turn around. Now let's see what damage the ship has suffered. Nice landing. No damage at all. Now to get this thing started again. I'll have to warm it up.*

Radam transmits, "Patrol 3 to Patrol Leader, I have you in sight. I am in the process of warming up before

90

ignition. No damage was taken on the landing. I get no life readings from the target area. The intruder is assumed terminated."

Patrol Leader inquires, "What happened to your voice Patrol 3?"

Radam is thinking, *Now I have him point blank. Goodbye, Leader. A direct hit. There should be three other ships and they would have been ordered into a triangular cover pattern. I can slip out without firing a shot. In the outer sectors, I'll be able to assemble a new raider band. No one will ever recognize me as Radam since the harsh climate on Duron has altered my appearance radically. Henceforth, I shall be known as Iceman.*

Chapter 10

Arrival On Vendra

Laar asks, "Well Ruther, now that we're on Vendra, who do we see?"

Ruther answers, "I don't know. Why don't we ask to see their leader."

Laar asks, "Are you sure they have one?"

Ruther answers, "They must have some kind of organization, so let's ask for their leader and hope it gets us some sort of positive response."

Laar asks, "Why don't we go to the police and ask them?"

Ruther agrees, "Good idea, Laar." Ruther suggests, "Let's go into that restaurant. We can get some food and ask the waitress where the police are located."

Laar changes the subject. "I wonder what kind of food they serve here."

Ruther answers, "There's only one way to find out. Grab a menu."

Laar says, "They have a good variety."

Ruther adds, "Their followers are from all over the galaxy. That could account for it."

Laar asks, "What are you having, Teena?"

Teena answers, "I think I'll choose from their vegetable selection."

Laar asks, "How about you, Ruther?"

Ruther observes, "They serve Kyne meat pie here. I haven't had that since I left Kyne. I hope they prepare it right."

Laar says, "I think I'll try some of their local seafood."

Ruther guesses, "It looks like we're supposed to punch in our selections. Which number was yours, Teena?"

Teena replies, "Eight."

Ruther adds, "Mine is fourteen."

Laar surmises, "I guess we just wait now."

Ruther suggests, "Why don't you punch in some drinks while we wait."

Laar agrees. "Good idea. I ordered a decanter of wine."

Teena observes, "Here it comes by robot."

Ruther interjects, "I don't think we're goin' to be able to ask anyone anythin' in here."

Laar says, "Everything seems very impersonal on this planet."

Ruther states, "I'd go crazy here. Let's finish up our business and get off this planet."

Laar adds sarcastically, "It was your idea to come here."

Ruther shoots back, "That's right, and as soon as we do what we came here to do, it's back to Lexicon."

Laar says, "I'm going to ask information from the first person we see."

Teena suggests, "Let's try the supply shop across the street."

Laar agrees, "Good idea, Teena."

Ruther changes the subject, "That was a good meal. The Kyne pie was perfect. I'll hit the finish button and get a robot over here with the check."

Laar gestures. "Now let's go across the street and get some information."

Ruther speaks, "Sir. We would like to know where the police are located."

The shopkeeper asks, "Has a crime been committed?"

Ruther replies, "No. But we need information, and the police can probably provide it."

The shopkeeper replies, "We have no police."

Ruther asks, "Who keeps order on this planet?"

The shopkeeper replies, "The members of the Order of the Universe."

Ruther inquires, "Where would we go to speak to one?"

The shopkeeper replies, "I am a member."

Ruther continues, "We have urgent information about an act that could be detrimental to universal balance."

The shopkeeper informs, "You must see the Trustees. They are in Central City. Take a shuttle to the city and have it drop you at the State House. You can tell the attendant what you told me, and he will set up an appointment for you. In the meantime, you will need a room."

Ruther says, "We don't intend to stay. As soon as we finish with our business, we are leavin'."

The shop keeper answers, "If the Trustees cannot see you immediately, you will need a place to stay. There is no place in Central City for visitors. I can reserve a room with dividers, so that you can all stay together."

Ruther inquires, "How much?"

The shopkeeper replies, "Ten notes apiece."

Ruther replies, "We'll take it. Where are the rooms?"

The shopkeeper replies, "At the inn next door. The room will only be reserved until seven o'clock, so be back before then."

Ruther suspiciously asks, "Why are you makin' the reservations? Do you get a commission?"

The shopkeeper answers, "I am the owner. I will call the front desk unless you want to go over and do it yourself."

Ruther relents. "No. Go ahead. Thanks."

Laar points. "Let's grab that shuttle."

Ruther mutters, "It's another pushbutton deal. I'll hit Central City. Then I'll hit State House. That should do it. Let's sit back and enjoy the sights."

Laar observes, "This planet has a lot of rivers."

Teens adds, "It's beautiful. Look, in the distance, that must be Central City."

Ruther adds, "It looks pretty large."

Teena points. "Look at those birds below us. We must be over a park of some sort. I'd love to go there. It looks peaceful and full of wildlife."

Laar suggests, "Maybe if we have time, Teena."

Ruther reminds them, "Don't forget what we're here for. This isn't a pleasure trip."

Teena snaps back, "Oh, Ruther. We can take some time to enjoy things before we leave."

Ruther backs off. "We'll see."

***

Ruther states, "This must be the place. Let's go in and get this over with."

The attendant asks, "Visitors. Who is it you wish to see?"

Ruther answers, "I don't know. We have some urgent information regarding the universal balance. A store owner sent us here."

The attendant states, "You will want to see the Trustees."

Ruther agrees, "Yes. The store owner mentioned the Trustees."

The attendant inquires, "Can you tell me the nature of your information?"

Ruther replies, "We know what caused those dead systems in Cotalion."

The attendant becomes serious. "This is most important. Let me see if the Trustees can be reached. Please wait here."

The attendant calls, "Can the Trustees be reached?"

The scheduler answers, "They are in conference."

The attendant asks, "Is anyone with them?"

The scheduler answers, "No."

The attendant interjects, "Then perhaps they can be interrupted."

The scheduler responds, "They have an appointment in half an hour."

The attendant replies, "This is important. Tell them that visitors are here with knowledge concerning the dead systems in Cotalion."

The scheduler replies, "I will relay your message."

The scheduler calls, "Excuse me, scholars. I have been advised that some visitors are in the lobby with information pertaining to the dead systems in Cotalion."

A Trustee replies, "Tell them that we will see them the first thing tomorrow. Have them here at nine o'clock. Thank you."

The scheduler tells the attendant, "Tell the visitors to be here at nine a.m. tomorrow."

Laar observes, "Here comes the guard."

The guard says, "Visitors. I am afraid that the Trustees cannot see you today. However, they wish to speak with you at nine a.m. tomorrow. Can you keep this appointment?"

Ruther urges, "We wanted to see them now so that we could complete our business and be on our way."

The guard answers, "I am sorry but that is impossible. They have a full schedule of appointments for today."

Ruther relents. "We'll return tomorrow. Let's go."

Teena suggests, "We have plenty of time to visit the park, Ruther. We already have a room."

Ruther concurs. "All right, Teena. Let's see what it's like."

***

The scheduler announces, "Trustees, the visitors are here as requested."

A Trustee replies, "Please send them in."

Ruther is astonished. "This room is incredible! Everythin' in it is one piece. It's like it was die cast. All metal. It glistens like nothin' I've ever seen before."

A Trustee gestures, "Please be seated. I see that you are astonished by this room. This is the Trustee Chamber. We each have our own living quarters off this chamber. This is where we live and work. You will notice that this chamber is covered by a dome. That is because this complex is a spacecraft capable of inter-galactic flight. That is why it is so constructed. But let us get to the business at hand."

The Trustee continues, "We were told that you have information regarding the dead systems in Cotalion. They are a mystery to us and are under our intense investigation. We have not been able to explain this phenomenon."

Ruther says emphatically, "Well, we can. The Realm is responsible. They have a weapon that causes the elements in a sun to react against themselves and to neutralize each other.

The Trustee replies, "This sounds impossible. We would have noticed it if there were weapons employed to cause the occurrences. And so would Cotalion."

Ruther disagrees. "No. They implanted a catalyst which caused the changes within the sun itself."

The Trustee inquires, "Without any change in mass? How did you learn about this?"

"I am Teena. I once worked as a companion on The Realm's major scientific research planet. I was sent to a man named Doctor Deemer. He is a cruel monster. As he tortured me, he boasted of a weapon he created that could destroy solar systems. I remembered his description of the weapon. He said that the weapon draws all of the energy of the object that it enters inward toward its center, creating a reaction that changes the composition of the object's interior without altering its mass or appearance. No outside energy source is used, so it is impossible to detect.

The Trustee is baffled. "Amazing! But how were you able to leave that planet?"

Teena replies, "I was sold to Lexicon, a vacation planet. That is where I am now licensed to work. I told my story to Laar, and he told Ruther. Ruther had always been interested in the dead systems. When Ruther found out, we came here to tell you. It was Ruther's idea to come."

The Trustee states, "We are grateful. You must become members of the Order of the Universe. Then you can help us put an end to this Realm threat. If you join, we will train you. Please consider Vendra as your new home. You are free to go but we need your help desperately.

Please think it over carefully. Tell us where you are staying so that we can contact you tomorrow for your decision. If you agree to join us, there will be a great deal for you to learn. That is why we need an answer so soon. Stay well."

***

Ruther grumbles, "Somehow this didn't turn out as expected. I thought we'd tell our story and be on our way."

Laar says, "Maybe that's what we should do, Ruther."

Ruther continues, "I don't know."

Laar asks, "Why should they need us?"

Ruther suggests, "I think we should find out before we decide. This could turn out to be a new start for us. Don't forget, we don't have our own ship anymore. Maybe there is somethin' here for us."

Laar says, "I'm willing to stay on, but how about Teena? We brought her out here, and I won't let her leave alone."

Teena speaks up, "Why must I leave Laar? I can live with you here as easily as on Lexicon."

Laar infers, "But your work and all your belongings?"

Teena replies, "They will keep. Besides, the park was so beautiful. More beautiful than anything on Lexicon. I am sure that there is much more on this planet. I would like to stay and see it all."

Laar asks, "Well, Ruther?"

Ruther responds, "I still want to hear what they have to say before we make our decision. But the way it looks,

I think we're goin' to be hangin' around. I just hope they have some good bars on this planet. You have Teena, but I'm still in need of companionship, and a lot of it. In fact, I'm goin' to ask our storekeeper friend where the action is on this planet. Don't wait up."

***

A Trustee speaks, "My fellow scholars. We must decide how to handle this new situation. There is more than one course possible. Let us now examine our choices.

"We can alert Cotalion of The Realm's actions. If we do that, we must be prepared to convince them that such a thing is really possible. If we are able to convince them of the possibility, we must then convince them that this is what actually occurred."

Another Trustee states, "We must find out the reason for The Realm's action. If we have a plausible reason, it will not be difficult to convince them."

Another Trustee replies, "Yes, but if we alert Cotalion, we are risking inter-galactic war. This could disrupt universal balance as much as The Realm's threat."

The Trustee agrees. "True. But we cannot attempt to stop The Realm by ourselves. We don't have the military might or the numbers to succeed."

Another Trustee answers, "We do have a greater technology. We can surely deal them a major blow. We can keep them off balance so that they will be forced to concentrate on us. This will prevent them from attacking Cotalion again."

The Trustee counters, "But only for as long as we are able to keep them occupied. It would only be a matter of time before we are defeated, and if we are defeated, there would be no one left to oppose The Realm."

Another Trustee suggests, "We could advise the Council of The Realm that we are wise to their actions and we can threaten to expose them if they use their weapon again."

The Trustee answers, "The Realm would never bow to such a threat, and this would not end the threat even if The Realm did desist. We would only hold them at bay for a time. It is more likely that The Realm would attack us. They would also fortify the borders to prevent us from crossing into Cotalion to alert them."

Another Trustee indicates, "The element of surprise is in our favor as long as The Realm is not aware that we have discovered their secret. It would be no problem for us to slip across the border as things stand now."

The presiding Trustee decides, "From what has been said, I find it necessary to provoke an inter-galactic war. It is the only way of ending The Realm threat completely. With our help, The Realm will fall to Cotalion for certain. We will make sure that both the inventor and the weapon are in our hands once The Realm is defeated. In that way the threat will disappear forever. There is far less of a threat to universal balance if our galaxy is conquered. At least the present threat, The Realm, will be eliminated."

***

Laar informs him, "Ruther, the Trustees are calling."

Ruther replies, "Let me talk to them."

"Good day, sirs."

The Trustee states, "We have called for your decision."

Ruther states, "Before I can answer you, I must know why you need our help so badly."

The Trustee responds, "If you join us, you will be trained in the knowledge of the Order of the Universe and prepared for a voyage to Cotalion."

Ruther is startled. "Cotalion? We don't even have a ship."

The Trustee continues, "We will supply the ship."

Ruther asks, "Why don't you send one of your members? They can convey the story as well as we can."

The Trustee replies, "Our membership lacks experienced space travelers. We have compiled information about your past. You were independent traders until your ship was confiscated in an unsuccessful attempt to cross the galactic border into Cotalion. You were willing to face the unknown then. After we train you, you will be far better prepared for the task. Between your knowledge and experience and what we shall teach you, your success is all but assured. We know little about the inhabitants of Cotalion beyond the fact that they are humanoid. We need your resourcefulness to accomplish our mission once you cross into Cotalion. Will you join us?"

Ruther asks, "Laar, Teena, what do you say?"

Laar responds, "We're in if you are."

Ruther responds, "That settles it then. We will join you."

The Trustee is delighted, "Splendid! You are to report for training at once. An instructor will meet you at the State House when you arrive. We thank you for your willingness to help and welcome you as future members of the Order. Stay well."

Ruther observes, "They seem to be in an awful hurry."

Laar responds, "There's no sense to keeping them waiting."

Chapter 11

The Training

"My name is Judith. I will be your instructor. You will be given the basic knowledge that is given to all members of the Order of the Universe. All members share a common belief. That belief is that nothing is more sacred than universal balance and stability. The Universe must be allowed to evolve through its own course, in its own time, and without any outside interference. The Order exists to gather knowledge and to preserve the universal balance. The only thing that separates one member from another is the personal experiences that he or she has been exposed to. This is what makes us our own being. In no other way should any member be different from another. All knowledge is to be shared. The Trustees possess no more knowledge than any other member. They gather all knowledge and see that it is disbursed throughout the membership. You will be asked to meet with the Trustees from time to time so that a transfer of knowledge may take place. Them to you, and you to them. Communication is essential if knowledge is to spread.

"This planet Vendra is the home of the Order. The Order is responsible for The Realm's quick victory during the last galactic war. We believed that this galaxy had to be ruled by one powerful government. We could not allow the war to continue for two major reasons. First, we could not allow the destruction of the ecologies of those planets where the fighting was taking place. Secondly, we could not allow each waring party to fight until they weakened each other to the point that the victor would be too weak to effectively control the galaxy. We did not wish to see a galaxy made up of small confederacies as in the past, or one infested with insurrection, anarchy, and piracy. This would not have been a healthy climate to promote universal balance. A choice had to be made between The Realm and its nemesis. We felt that The Realm forces were stronger, and their leaders were superior. For this reason, we secretly aided The Realm without advising them of our support. We engineered the final battle in Sector C8. By a series of counterfeit transmissions that we allowed each side to intercept, we set the scene for that final decisive battle. We did not allow any Realm ships to be destroyed, so that they would emerge the victor and be at full strength after they crushed the enemy.

Laar speaks. "I have a question, Judith."

Judith acknowledges him. "What is it, Laar?"

Laar asks, "How did the Order accomplish it?"

Judith answers, "We rendered the enemy ships powerless. They were unable to maneuver or discharge their weapons."

Laar questions, "But how?"

Judith explains, "We studied the computer systems employed by their ships. They were similar to, but not the same as those used in The Realm's ships. We were able to take control of their systems by using a stronger signal that we transmitted from our post here on Vendra. We simply shut down all of their systems. That is why we are here on Vendra. We needed an uninhabited planet, far from normal trade vectors, where we could construct the enormous transmitter and control center needed to accomplish our task. This same system has been adapted to be used against The Realm if they should attempt to attack Vendra and destroy the Order. We have been safe here on Vendra ever since. The Order has flourished and our technology along with us. Our technology far surpasses that of The Realm, as you shall learn. That is because we learn and share our knowledge and we are not preoccupied with material gain.

"A great deal of knowledge can be obtained through observation. We will teach you how to always be alert, even while you relax. This will be one of your most important lessons. When you believe that there is nothing at all happening, you are in error. There is always something happening around you. The Universe is never still. Because your senses cannot perceive something, it doesn't mean it doesn't exist. Your training will sharpen your senses, but even at their best, they will never be able to perceive more than a small fraction of what is surrounding you at any given moment. This is why you must understand the Universe and its rhythm. Between your senses and your knowledge and understanding, you will be alert at all times to what is happening to you and around you. You will never be caught by surprise. This all sounds abstract, but it will be your first basic lesson. It will take time to perfect, but it will become second nature to you, as it has to all of our members.

"You will be fully trained in the functioning of your body. All of its basic mechanics will become a part of your knowledge. I will teach you the basic mechanics of the Universe as well. The knowledge of the two together will allow you to perform tasks that would now seem impossible to you. Your training will teach you to analyze, synthesize, and formulate rapidly in any situation. Your trained mind will show you ways of doing things that an untrained mind would not conceive. You will be more than a match for any person or machine or any combination of the two."

Laar asks, "Question, Judith. Haven't any members ever used their training in unethical ways?"

Judith responds, "That is impossible as you shall learn. Once you have the knowledge that we provide, it will be totally unnatural for you to think along unethical lines. You will see the folly in such actions. You will become a master of yourself and a servant of the universe.

"You will learn about weapons. How to use them and how to neutralize their effects. This knowledge is essential, although you will rarely, if ever, use a weapon. Your body is the most effective weapon you possess. It has very limited range, but if anything is out of its range, it can be dealt with by other means. Confrontation is not always the way to victory. Everything in the universe is vulnerable to something, but it has been given the means to protect itself against its vulnerabilities. Only artificially induced forces can prevent this balance from working. The Order must protect this balance at all times. The Universe is naturally in balance. It must not be altered or interfered with.

"Your training will familiarize you with every culture, race, and religion within the galaxy. You will learn the basic beliefs and the origins of each. You will also be exposed to the ethnic art forms and music of each. You will understand their architecture by deduction, as architecture is a product of environment and resources, influenced esthetically by culture. You will be able to assimilate comfortably on any inhabited planet in the galaxy once you learn this lesson.

"You will study the plant and animal life that is found throughout the galaxy. You will learn their evolution, capabilities, interaction with one another, and the environment. You will learn their temperament and tendencies. You will learn their diets and commercial uses if they have any. You will become proficient botanists and zoologists before your training is complete.

"After you have sufficient mastery of the knowledge taught to you, you will be exposed to the practical applications of our technology. Remember, your general knowledge is never complete. You will add to it every day and those things that you learn will become more and more ingrained until they are second nature to you. Let us now formally begin your training."

Judith speaks. "You have learned a great deal in the months you have spent with me. You have been diligent, and it has been my pleasure to instruct you. You are, in my estimation, ready for your technical training. For this you will have a new instructor. Lila will take over the responsibility of the remainder of your training. The next time we meet, it will be as friends. I am not to be thought of as your teacher any longer. Stay well, friends."

Teena requests, "Leave us your home code, Judith. We will contact you the first chance we get."

"Students, I am Lila. I will teach you things you never thought existed. You will also learn to do things you never thought possible.

Lila continues, "You will now be given a suit that is identical to that worn by all members of the Order. You may choose any color you desire, but the suit may not be altered in any way. You will be fitted for your suits immediately. After they are fitted, they will be removed immediately. You will understand why later. You are to return to me with your suits as soon as the fitting is completed. Be sure not to wear the suits before you return to me. Go now."

Lila speaks. "You are now ready to begin your final training phase. I will start you off with the truth. There is no such being as a super humanoid. There is such a thing as a humanoid developed to the fullest extent of his physical and mental capabilities. You will become such a being, as have all other members of the Order. The human species can be awesome when developed. I will develop you.

"Now I want you to try and grab me. You first, Ruther."

Ruther is astonished, "That's impossible. How did you move so fast?"

Lila continues, "Now you, Laar. Now both of you together. Join in, Teena."

Laar is amazed. "How do you do it? Human reflexes are not that fast. You move faster than a machine."

Lila replies, "Technology, friends. One of the greatest human characteristics is the ability to develop tools and use them to accomplish tasks that would otherwise be impossible. This suit that I am wearing is a tool. It is a product of our technology. We used our knowledge of our bodies and the properties of elements to develop a synthetic fabric that once fitted to your musculature, magnifies any muscular response. The fabric acts in an opposite manner from rubber. When rubber is stretched, it springs back to its original form. When this fabric is stretched by the expansion or contraction of your muscles, it springs to change its form to conform to your body. The combination of your reflexes and the response of the fabric enables you to react instantly at a speed not even the fastest machine will be able to match.

"You must learn to control your suit. That is why I cautioned you against wearing it right now. If you move in your normal manner, the suit will send you out of control. You will learn to refine your movements and obtain the same results with a fraction of the energy expenditure you would need if were not wearing the suit. It will become necessary for you to exercise often with your suits off in order to prevent your muscles from degenerating. While your suit is on, your muscles don't have to work. Eventually they will weaken and all the benefits gained by wearing the suit will be lost because your reflexes will slow due to loss of muscle tone.

"Now we will do a series of slow-motion exercises. This is the speed you must keep while wearing your suit. This speed will allow you to move at a normal pace. It will feel natural once you have your suits on. Right now, it is a strain for you to move at this slow rate. You will now go and put on your suits. Remember, move only as you did during our exercise session. You will be amazed at the result."

***

Lila speaks. "Now that you feel natural in your suits, you are ready for the next lesson. For inter-planetary travel, we have developed a new propulsion system. We refer to it as

Bounce Drive. It works on the principle of attraction and repulsion. As you know, all solid things have mass. The bottom of our spacecraft is an energy projection disc. The generator inside the craft can produce a variety of energy fields. It can produce fields that both attract and repel. The intensity of the field is adjustable. To take off, the craft is set to repel. The intensity of the field will determine your thrust and eventual speed. Once you leave a planet's atmosphere, you will maintain your speed until you modify it. It can be modified by either attracting or repelling against the next object you encounter. The craft is equipped with a conventional engine so that you can maneuver in space where no object is within range of the energy generator. You must use your conventional engine sparingly because your fuel storage is very limited. Do not rely on it. If you master our flight technology, you will never need to use the emergency engine. In order to land, you will use the repel mode to slow down and the attract mode to bring you in at your desired landing speed. Once you master the technique, you will be able to land the craft without so much as a bump. You can set your energy transmission to attract if you want to tow an object or have it tow you. You can determine direction by adjusting the position of the energy disc. If you are not in range of an object and you want to change direction, you can release some of the pressure from the guidance valves. This will create enough push to alter your direction.

"The advantages to our propulsion system are numerous. Our method offers greater control, enables far greater speeds, makes no noise or fuel trail, and greatest of all, requires no fuel. You can travel virtually indefinitely and if pursued, never need to make a stop.

"You are already fine navigators from past experiences, so there is no need for me to teach this to you. Teena can learn from you. Her navigation education is in your hands. Now it is a matter of mastering the controls and flight techniques of the craft. We shall now board the ship."

***

Lila concludes, "You have mastered the mechanics of the spacecraft. The rest of your technological training will be academic. You have completed the practical applications and are ready to take your place among the members of the Order. You are as I am. We are all in the service of the Universe. You are well trained, but never forget that your learning never ceases. There is something to be learned in everything you do. You are now trained to take advantage of this fact to the fullest. Never feel that you are superior to another. Everyone has the same capabilities. It is the degree of development that governs performance. If you are not certain of an individual's training and knowledge, it is best not to underestimate that person.

"I will report the completion of your required training to the Trustees. You will be assimilated into our society with the aid of the Trustees. You will be given your choice of residence and social functions. From then on, your time is yours. Live well."

Ruther, Laar, and Teena say in unison, "Live well, Lila."

Chapter 12

The Mission

The Trustee speaks. "We are delighted that you have joined the Order. You were informed of the mission before you had underwent your training. A great deal of time has passed since then. We ask if you still wish to participate and fulfill the mission."

Ruther replies, "We are prepared and realize that the probability of success is heavily in our favor. When does the mission begin?"

The Trustee answers, "A ship has been prepared. You are stocked with food enough to sustain you there and back, barring the unforeseen. The only caution we shall give is to be careful of the border traps. You can detect them by projecting your energy field ahead of you like a probe. If your energy field is dampened ahead of you, you will know not to cross at that point. Use a very weak field to probe so that contact with the trap will not be detected.

"Live well. We will await your return."

***

Ruther is impressed, "This ship is without a doubt superior to anythin' The Realm has. We can't miss with a ship like this."

Laar acknowledges, "You were right, Ruther. The Order is no myth. We will defeat The Realm. By the time we return, our members will be strategically planted to initiate the internal upheaval. The forces of Cotalion should have little trouble after that."

Teena states, "Well, I think we should enjoy this part of the mission. We don't have any worries for another twelve l-days. We won't run into any border patrols until then."

Ruther answers enthusiastically, "Right you are, Teena. Party time. Break out the Vendran Red. The Order sure knows how to make fine wine. They have mastered the art."

Laar quips, "You should know."

***

Ruther states, "We've been out here eleven l-days. It's time to pick a spot and head for it. Any suggestions?"

Laar suggests, "Why don't we try between the Minter System and the Frontis System?"

Ruther adds, "That's the narrowest passage between any of the major systems in this sector."

Laar agrees. "I know. Chances are, they will have fewer patrol ships assigned to cover this area. They may not even have any border traps since the area is easier to patrol."

Ruther adds, "We would have a lot more maneuverin' room between Corda and Vale."

Laar counters, "I'm just afraid they'll have a lot of traps in that area because the area is much larger to patrol."

Ruther relents. "Makes sense. Between Minter and Frontis it is."

Laar gestures. "Let's go."

Ruther inquires, "Anythin on the screen, Laar?"

Laar answers, "There are a couple ships off port about 20 l-minutes from us. There seems to be a lot of activity around Frontis 5 too. I think we should parallel the border at our maximum field projection and probe for traps."

Ruther says, "Slow us down so we don't arouse too much suspicion. When we find an openin', chart it and head for the nearest planet."

Laar is alert. "We attracted attention. Four ships are closing in at intercept speed."

Ruther asks, "Did you find an openin' yet?"

Laar answers, "No."

Ruther suggests, "Make a wide arc and head for Minter 3. That'll give you a little more time to probe."

Laar advises, "The ships are veering off. The course change must have satisfied them."

Ruther is relieved, "Good."

Laar shouts, "Wait! I found an opening!"

Ruther says, "All right. Slow us down and keep our present course. As soon as those patrols clear the area, we'll hit a bounce point and get up as much speed as we can. What planet is nearest to the openin'?"

Laar answers, "Minter 7."

Ruther says, "Let me know when the area is clear."

Laar says, "Okay."

Ruther orders, "Change course and head full speed for Minter 7. Now! We're goin' to bounce off Minter 7 at full intensity repel. We'll bounce off so fast that no ship'll get within firin' range of us. Strap in. This'll be some jolt."

Teena is concerned. "Is everyone okay?"

Laar responds, "I'm fine, Teena. How about you Ruther?"

Ruther gasps, "What a shot! How fast are we goin'?"

Laar states, "We'll be across the border in less than half an l-hour."

Ruther blurts, "Incredible."

Teena counters, "Nothing is incredible anymore."

Ruther agrees. "Right you are, Teena."

Teena adds, "We surprised the stars out of those patrols. They're trying to pursue us, but they may as well be standing still."

Laar adds, "It looks like we made it."

Ruther acknowledges him. "We'll soon know for sure. We're approaching the border. Don't slow down until we cross and put some distance between us and the border."

Laar exclaims, "We're across!"

Ruther roars, "Teena, break out the wine."

Laar cautions, "Take it easy, Ruther. We don't know what to expect now that we're in Cotalion. We'd better stay alert from now on."

Ruther responds, "One glass in celebration won't hurt."

Laar concedes. "Okay, Ruther. We'll join you with one glass."

***

Laar states, "There's a system about two l-days ahead."

Ruther responds, "We're here to contact someone, so we'd better head for it."

Laar adds, "I'm surprised we haven't been intercepted."

Ruther quips, "I guess they weren't expectin' us."

Laar continues, "Very funny. If we entered Stasis, we'd sure be met by a greeting party."

Ruther says, "Maybe these Cotalions are peaceful."

Laar continues, "We'll see how peaceful they are when they hear our story. Wait, I'm picking up some activity on my screen."

Ruther asks, "What kind of activity?"

Laar responds, "Ships. Looks like a carrier and its escort. There are five ships headed toward us at intercept speed."

Ruther mutters, "I was waitin' for this. Peaceful, like hell. Send out a greetin' and see if they respond."

Laar blurts, "No response."

Ruther hesitantly says, "I hope they understood the message."

Laar says, "All I know is that they're still coming. Should we evade them?"

Ruther asks, "Can we?"

Laar responds, "Not for long without a bounce."

Ruther quips, "Well, slow down and stay on course. Just hope they take us prisoner instead of blowin' us away."

Laar speculates, "If we don't show fear or hostility, we should be all right."

Ruther is tense. "Well, we'll soon find out."

Laar agrees. "You're right, we're surrounded."

Ruther adds, "At least they didn't fire at us. I don't understand why they don't attempt to contact us."

Laar says, "They're just escorting us in."

The Cotalion officer orders, "Identify yourself."

Ruther blurts, "Well, answer them."

Laar states nervously, "We never named the ship."

Ruther blurts, "Call it *Ibex* 2."

Laar responds, "This is *Ibex* 2."

The Cotalion officer demands, "What is your point of origin?"

Laar responds, "We are from Planet Vendra in the Stasia Galaxy."

The Cotalion officer bellows, "You are invaders."

Laar quickly counters, "We have come alone with information of a highly sensitive nature."

The Cotalion officer orders, "Stay on your present course. We will escort you to our carrier where you will surrender your ship."

Laar states, "We wish to speak to your commander."

The Cotalion officer advises, "You will have no choice. He will surely interrogate you."

Laar answers, "We will surrender."

The Cotalion officer continues, "You will be given landing instructions as we approach the carrier. How many are aboard your vessel?"

Laar answers, "Three."

Ruther gestures, "Let's put our suits on. We may need them."

The Cotalion officer orders, "You will now begin your landing."

Ruther quips, "Well, we're all theirs now."

The Cotalion officer continues, "You will now disembark. Follow me. You will be placed in confinement until the commander is free to see you. Guard, provide the prisoners with refreshment."

Ruther mutters, "They seem civilized."

Laar observes, "They certainly aren't primitive. Not from what I've seen of their ships and the size of this carrier."

Laar adds, "I wonder how long it will take the commander to arrive."

Ruther responds, "He's probably in no hurry. To tell you the truth, neither am I. At least these refreshments are good."

Ruther adds, "Hey look. They're openin' the door."

The Cotalion officer commands, "You will come with me. The commander wishes to see you in one of the conference rooms. Enter and be seated."

"Commander, these are the prisoners."

"I am Admiral Tele of the United Cotalion Empire. I command this fleet which is the main body of the Cotalion/Stasia Border Force. Your ship is an unknown design to us. We have never encountered such a ship in our prior contact with your galaxy. We believed our technologies equal until now."

Ruther answers, "Our ship is a special vessel, Admiral. We are members of a group called the Order of the Universe. We stand for universal balance and are pledged to preserve it at all costs. We are a small autonomous group. We are separate from The Realm."

Admiral Tele asks, "The Realm. What is that?"

Laar answers, "The Realm is the ruling government in Stasia. Only the Order possesses the advanced technology to build a ship such as ours. Our advanced technology is what has enabled us to remain autonomous. We have been able to stalemate The Realm by remaining on our home planet Vendra and shielding it against attack. The Realm wasted too much time and resources trying to subjugate us, so they gave up. We don't give them any reason to attack us, so they leave us alone."

Admiral Tele inquires, "Why did you come to Cotalion?"

Ruther answers, "We have information of the most urgent nature. It concerns the dead solar systems in your galaxy."

Admiral Tele asks, "What do you know about them?"

Ruther answers, "We know the cause."

Admiral Tele warns, "If this is some trick to gain your freedom, it will cost you your lives."

Ruther assures him, "It's no trick."

Admiral Tele orders, "Guards, leave the room and stand guard outside the door. Now speak."

Ruther continues, "The Realm has created a weapon that destroyed the suns in your dead systems."

Admiral Tele blurts, "Nonsense."

Ruther quickly responds. "No, listen. Here is how it works. The device draws the sun's energy inward toward its center and is the catalyst to a reaction that alters the composition of the sun's interior without changin' its mass or appearance. The sun is destroyed from within by its own energy. No outside energy is needed and no change of appearance occurs, makin' it impossible to detect."

Admiral Tele is skeptical. "This is hard to believe. How was this device placed? We detected no alien ships in Cotalion, but there were three instances where we pursued unidentified ships toward Stasia, but they self-destructed before we could reach them. We still do not know their origin."

Ruther admits, "We don't know how the devices were planted or why, but we know The Realm is behind it."

Admiral Tele further inquires, "Why do you come to us with this information?"

Ruther explains, "The Order is pledged to preserve universal balance. The weapon can destroy that balance forever. It has already disrupted it in the case of your dead systems. The Order has the technology to defeat The Realm but we don't have the manpower or resources to do it. That is why we are here. We will aid Cotalion in defeating The Realm. We will disrupt them internally and occupy as many of their forces as we can in the inner galaxy. That will make it easier for you to invade Stasia."

Admiral Tele responds. "I will relay this information to the First Councilman. He must decide what to do. You will be sent back to detention until I am given further orders. You will be afforded all possible comforts in the meantime.

"Guards, return them to detention.

"We will speak again."

Laar asks, "Do you think he believed us?"

Ruther replies, "I don't really care about him. I hope the First Councilman believes us."

Laar adds, "If he doesn't, we're a long way from home."

Ruther quips, "Relax. We'll make it back no matter what."

***

Admiral Tele speaks. "The First Councilman has accepted your story as truth. He considers the incidents an act of war no matter what the reason. He intends to make The Realm pay for their crime. An immediate attack will be launched against The Realm. You are free to go. We will supply you with whatever you may need for your journey."

Ruther blurts, "Wait! Didn't you tell the First Councilman that we will help you?"

Admiral Tele replies, "Yes. But he does not believe we require your help."

Ruther exclaims, "That is foolish. He knows nothing about The Realm."

Admiral Tele replies sternly, "We have a vast and powerful fleet and our troops are well trained and well equipped. We have been standing ready to protect our trade vessels in Stasia in the event that they were attacked."

Ruther argues, "Well, what does he think The Realm has? They control a galaxy too. Even if you defeat The Realm, chances are you'll be left so weak after the war that you won't be able to control either galaxy effectively. We can't permit such instability to occur."

Admiral Tele bellows, "You have no say in the matter."

Ruther implores, "Please, let us speak to the First Councilman. We can save you time, lives, and resources. We ask nothin' but our continued freedom in return. You, as a military man must understand the advantage of an internal ally. Convince the First Councilman to talk to us."

Admiral Tele relents. "I will try. I have some influence with him, especially concerning military matters. You wait. In the meantime, is there anything you need for your return journey?"

Laar replies, "If your fuel is the same as ours, we would like our supply replenished."

Admiral Tele replies, "It is similar enough. We will take care of that. Is there anything else?"

"Then wait for my return."

***

Admiral Tele returns. "I have spoken to the First Councilman. He is willing to hold the attack and accept your aid."

Ruther exclaims, "Thank the stars!"

Admiral Tele continues, "Now we must discuss strategy. Let's go into one of the conference rooms. There we will have star charts at our disposal if needed. I have been given the high command for this invasion. Its ultimate success or failure is now my responsibility entirely. I have called in the twenty-nine other fleet commanders and put them on war alert status. They are now awaiting my orders."

Ruther explains, "They will have to wait awhile. It will take time to draw The Realm's forces into the center of the galaxy. We will return to Vendra at top speed to save as much time as possible. But our part will take time. You must be patient."

Admiral Tele asks, "How will we communicate? Transmission from Cotalion to Stasia can be detected."

Ruther mutters, "Shuttlin' back and forth will be too time consumin' and risky.

Admiral Tele exclaims, "Wait. We have been entering your galaxy to buy food and your Realm has made no effort to stop us. We can exchange information through our traders. We will place agents aboard our cargo vessels to act as liaisons."

Ruther agrees. "Excellent idea. We have a friend who is a Lander on one of the planets where you trade. His name is Cholly. He is on Meris. We will use Meris as our communication place. I will show you where it is on the star charts."

Admiral Tele concurs. "It is in a good location. Not too far from the border. Messages can be relayed quickly from there."

Ruther advises, "Continue your trade as usual. When the internal disturbances have accomplished their purpose, we will tell you that the time is right. From then on, the strategy is yours. We will leave you now."

Admiral Tele adds, "Before you leave, I want you to meet the agents who will communicate with you on Meris. In that way we will minimize the chance of error or discovery."

Chapter 13

Diversion

The attendant declares, "Teena, Ruther, and Laar have returned from Cotalion."

The Trustee responds, "Please send them in."

Ruther announces, "We have good news. Cotalion is willing to participate. They will wait for our signal before mounting an invasion."

The Trustee asks, "Have you told them our plan?"

Ruther replies, "Yes. We are supposed to communicate with them by relaying messages through their agents who will be on cargo ships trading with Meris."

The Trustee says, "Good."

Ruther continues, "We met the agents who we will be dealing with."

The Trustee suggests, "Since you know them, I think you should be the ones to relay the messages to them. You will go to Meris and take an apartment there. We will send messengers to you, and you will relay the information. You must leave immediately. All other agents are in position."

A conspirator speaks. "I have just received word from Vendra. The day has come. We must now take steps to initiate the war. As planned, we will begin the systematic disruption on the capital planet. The first step will be to cut off all communication between the capital and the rest of The Realm. Once this has been accomplished, we will begin our attacks on the military installations in an attempt to keep them off balance. After we have sufficiently harassed the military, we will allow them to find our dummy headquarters and lull them into believing that they have crushed the uprising. By then, we will have sent word to the other planets to begin their phase of the plan and disrupt the economies on the other planets through acts of sabotage. The military will be disbursed to the various planets to restore control. Once this occurs, we will resurface on the capital and cut off communication as before. It will become our task to keep as much of the military as we can right here on the capital planet. As the planetary disruptions expand, the military will be drawn in toward the inner planets where the trouble is occurring. They will leave the outer systems undermanned. Once we accomplish this, we will send word to Vendra that the time is right for Cotalion to launch their attack."

Ruther exclaims, "I never thought I'd see this day. The Realm is goin' to crumble."

Laar agrees, "Hard to believe."

Ruther asks, "Teena, do you feel up to relievin' Laar for a while? I'm pretty tired and I know Laar has been at the helm too long."

Teena assures them, "Sure. I'll be able to handle the ship."

Ruther directs her, "Good. Lay in a course for Meris."

***

The Trustee speaks. "Phase one is completed. Our agents have struck on hundreds of planets. The Realm doesn't know where to send its troops first. They are beginning to pull troops from the outer sectors to try to restore order."

Another Trustee replies, "Good. Now that the outer sectors are under fortified, we will put phase two into motion to ensure that the military continues to concentrate on the inner planets. When the time is right, we will signal the invasion and take the outer planets before they know what has hit them. In the meantime, we will have our agents hijack as many of their warships as they can and use some of their own weapons against them."

***

A pirate asks, "Iceman, do you have any idea about what is going on?"

Iceman replies, "It appears to be some sort of revolution. This is our opportunity to expand our raids throughout the outer sectors. They are decreasing their patrols as they send ships to the inner sectors to put down the revolt. I want our pirates active. Attack anything with Realm markings. Nothing would please me better than to see The Realm destroyed. We'll disrupt trade so badly that the outer planets will rebel too, when they don't get the protection they expect. You men keep the notes and supplies pouring in. I'm taking my craft to attack the military. I'm going to make things difficult for those fighters. I'll hit and run them until they are afraid to take off. I can out fly any space fighter they have. We will get rich and blast The Realm at the same time. Let's go men. Our time has come."

***

The Director orders, "Brodis, report to me at once. I must know what is happening."

Brodis replies, "On my way, Director."

The Director is puzzled. "I don't understand it. Everything was under complete control, and now without warning, I have a rebellion. Not just on one planet, but all over the heart of The Realm. I should have been given some sort of warning. I need answers fast. This rebellion is very organized. We are having trouble controlling it. They are a well-coordinated group. I must know who the organizer is. I can stop them at their source if I know the organizer."

The guard announces, "Director, Brodis is here."

The Director orders, "Send him in and be sure we are not disturbed."

Brodis states, "I think I know why I'm here."

The Director is agitated, "What do you know about this rebellion? Who are they? What do they want?"

Brodis replies, "I have had my men investigating the incidents as they spring up. So far, we have been unable to catch them or trace them. I have no information yet."

The Director shouts, "You'd better get some fast. I want this rebellion crushed before it spreads any further. We have been forced to draw our forces into the inner sectors to help get this under control. The pirates are already taking advantage of the situation."

Brodis speculates, "They may be the group behind the rebellion."

The Director bellows, "Nonsense. When have you ever known pirates to be so organized?"

Brodis replies, "Never before, but this Iceman has some reputation in the outer sectors. He has formed a formidable band of pirates. Maybe he has become the pirate leader for the whole galaxy."

The Director responds, "Knowing pirates as I do, that is not likely. But speaking of this Iceman, he has become extremely bold. He is personally attacking our military vessels. He has already destroyed over a dozen fighters. I wonder who he is? He is certainly as good a warrior as any of our finest fighter pilots, maybe better based on recent encounters. As soon as we put down this rebellion, I want him dead, and his body brought to me. I want to see what sort of man he is. But back to the rebellion."

Brodis relates, "I have heard stories that Icemen crashed on a frozen planet when he was a child, and that he was the sole survivor of the crash. He raised himself until a pirate ship that landed for repairs picked him up."

The Director barks, "I'm not interested in any stories. I want facts about the rebellion. What do you know, Brodis?"

Brodis replies, "The rebellion began like a wave. It started here on the capital planet and spread outward in circles. This pattern conforms with the distance it takes for inter-planetary communication. It is as though the signal was sent in all directions from here, and as each planet received the signal, it joined the rebellion. Very organized."

The Director states, "We aren't dealing with any isolated fools."

Brodis agrees. "No. On the contrary, this was planned in great detail."

The Director inquires, "Why did they choose now to begin? We are in our strongest military position since the formation of The Realm."

Brodis agrees, "Yes, and we get stronger all the time. Maybe they felt that they needed to strike before we became any stronger."

The Director asks, "If that is the case, why didn't they strike sooner?"

Brodis replies, "Maybe they weren't prepared until now."

The Director is agitated. "All I know is that they are disrupting the very core of The Realm and that we have been unable to stop it. We must find out who they are so we can attack the source. We cannot fight a terrorist war. It could go on forever. We can't afford to tie up our troops for extended periods without jeopardizing the stability of the outer sectors. We can't afford to leave the inner sectors at the mercy of terrorists either. The economic stability of The Realm depends on smooth administration from within. If the inner planets are disrupted, the entire Realm will sink into turmoil. We must stop this rebellion now."

Brodis responds, "The only advice I have is to concentrate our forces and make a planet-by-planet cleanup until we have more information about the source. It won't yield an immediate end, but at least it will show that we are taking positive action. If we can clean up a few planets, it will show that we are making progress."

The Director replies, "Well, I'll get my generals to clean up this planet first. But in the meantime, I want you to tell me who they are. Get to it!"

Brodis answers, "Yes, Director. Immediately."

***

The Trustee speaks. "Now is the time. They have concentrated their forces against our attacks. They are stopping our raids one planet at a time. We must get the invasion under way before any more of our members are sacrificed. Once the invasion starts, they'll be forced to suspend their present actions in order to meet the new threat. Once they do that, we'll combine forces into a unified strike force, and with the equipment we've already captured we'll overwhelm a base and get our army fully equipped for an all-out offensive. We will push from the interior while the invasion pushes from the outer sectors. The Realm will be caught in a two-front war, unable to concentrate their forces. We will meet the invasion fleet and cut The Realm in two. Send word to Ruther, Laar, and Teena on Meris. They must advise Cotalion."

***

Laar says, "Things must be heating up by now. I think I'll go to see Cholly tonight. We'll have to take him with us when the time comes. I'll try to convince him to come with us."

Ruther agrees, "Good idea, Laar. I don't know what you'll tell him, but if you can convince him, it is for his own good."

Laar says, "I hope Cholly is home. If not, I'll try at A Piece of Paradise."

Cholly is surprised, "Laar, what are you doing here? When did you land?"

Laar replies, "We came in recently."

Cholly inquires, "Are you here to trade again? Come on in. Fill me in on what's new with you and Ruther. Want a drink?"

Laar replies, "Sure. I came over to ask you something. We want to know if you have some vacation time that you can take."

Cholly inquires, "What do you have in mind?"

Laar responds, "We had a good run in the mining systems and were able to buy a new larger ship. We call it Ibex 2. It's a real fine craft. Anyway, I met a girl named Teena on Lexicon and we're going to unite."

Cholly shouts, "Congratulations, Laar. All the best."

Laar replies, "Thanks. But I want you to come along with us so you can attend the ceremony."

Cholly is excited. "I wouldn't miss it for all the stars. When are you leaving?"

Laar says, "Any day now. The ship is being overhauled, and as soon as it's ready, we'll leave."

Cholly continues, "Okay. I'll give notice tomorrow. Why don't you call Ruther and Teena and we'll all go out and celebrate. Meanwhile, I'll get ready."

Laar calls. "Ruther, get Teena to come to the viewer."

Ruther tells Teena, "Laar wants to talk to both of us."

Laar speaks. "Listen, I told Cholly that Teena and I were going to unite on Lexicon. He agreed to take some time off and come with us for the ceremony."

Ruther says, "Good thinkin', Laar."

Laar continues, "Cholly wants to go out and celebrate, so why don't you both come over."

Ruther replies, "We'll see you in a few minutes."

***

An agent alerts them. "Ruther, the Trustees say that it is time for the invasion. Pass the word."

Ruther replies, "Right away. Stay well."

137

"Laar, contact Cholly. We must leave as soon as possible. Once the message is relayed, the invasion will begin. It will only take a few days for this planet to be taken. We must be gone before then.

"Teena, you will contact the agent while me and Laar prepare the ship."

Teena motions, "I'm on my way."

Laar says, "I'll call Cholly now."

"Cholly, this is Laar. How soon can you be ready to leave?"

Cholly asks, "Is your ship ready?"

Laar says, "Yes."

Cholly replies, "I'll be ready tomorrow morning then."

Laar says, "Good. Meet us at Port 42."

Cholly affirms, "See you tomorrow."

Laar advises, "That's it, Ruther. Let's get started on the *Ibex*. We'll leave tomorrow morning when Cholly gets here."

***

A messenger announces, "Admiral Tele. The word has been given. It is time to attack."

Admiral Tele replies, "Thank you, messenger. I have been waiting for this moment. Open all channels to the fleet commanders.

"This is Tele. Let the invasion begin. I repeat, let the invasion begin. Keep the lines of communication open at all times. Send the cargo ships carrying our troops down to the planets that we have been trading with. Upon arrival, the troops will disburse and secure the planets as planned. The planets, once secured, are to be prepared for our fleet arrivals. We will attack from these bases. The occupation must be swift. The fleets will only be one day behind. All fleets will move into position and advance according to the timetable. Are all cargo ships away?"

The commanders reply, "Yes, Admiral."

Admiral Tele continues, "Then the timetable starts from now. We will follow the primary plan. The initial seven fleets will advance to our newly designated bases. Two of the seven will advance deeper into Stasia with a distance five l-Days between them and the midpoint system that has been designated. The other five fleets will protect the assigned areas and cover our bases. The two advanced fleets will continue ahead, engaging anything in their path. When we have determined the enemy's formation and the strength of their resistance, we will advance three of the back five fleets. By this time, the remaining ten invasion fleets will have begun their advance to the secured bases. They will advance two fleets at a time. The first two to arrive will station themselves to protect the bases in the areas vacated by the previous three fleets. The remaining eight fleets will be directed where needed. I expect the enemy to concentrate on repelling the invasion. When they fortify their defenses, we will encounter our heaviest fighting. But before they can fully fortify, our allies in the interior sectors will attack from the rear and flanks. The Realm will be caught between forces and will not be able to concentrate their forces. This should allow our combined forces to deliver a decisive blow. If the allies are successful, we should meet them at some point. Once we meet, we will have driven a wedge and cut The Realm in half. Once this is accomplished, the outer sectors will begin to realize that no help will be coming and they will begin to surrender. With The Realm cut in half, it will be difficult for The Realm's remaining fleets to mount a combined attack. Then it is just a matter of time. The occupation troops will follow our fleets and occupy the defeated planets that are left in our wake. The Realm will regret the day they began destroying our systems. If we are fortunate, we may even capture the criminals who ordered the atrocities.

"Fellow Commanders, pour yourselves a drink. Let us drink a toast to victory for our fleets and the destruction of The Realm."

***

Cholly observes, "Hey, Laar! Where are you flying? Lexicon is in the interior. You're flying parallel to Lexicon."

Ruther responds, "Well, Cholly. Now is as good a time as any to explain."

Cholly is confused. "Explain what?"

Ruther gestures. "Relax and listen. Stasia is bein' invaded by Cotalion."

140

Cholly is surprised. "What?"

Ruther continues, "Listen. By tomorrow, Meris will be in Cotalion hands. We had to get you out of there so you wouldn't get hurt."

Cholly snaps, "Have you been drinking, Ruther?"

Laar adds, "It's true, Cholly."

Choly inquires, "What is this all about and how did you find out about it?"

Laar continues, "Teena found out that The Realm caused the dead solar systems in Cotalion. Ruther felt that someone else should know. We went to Vendra and told the story to the Trustees of the Order of the Universe."

Cholly is annoyed. "Those hermits. Why?"

Laar continues, "Ruther felt that they could prevent any further atrocities by The Realm. He was right. We joined the Order and are part of the action being taken against The Realm."

Cholly, in disbelief, says, "I know you had no allegiance to The Realm, but I never thought you were traitors."

Ruther says, "You can't be a traitor against somethin' that you have no allegiance to."

Cholly yells, "You're as bad as a revolutionary or a pirate."

Ruther asks, "Do you condone what The Realm has done?"

Cholly answers, "I don't believe it. You sold out an entire galaxy."

Ruther is disappointed. "I'm sorry you feel that way."

Cholly screams, "I'll kill you!"

Laar says, "You didn't have to hit him, Ruther."

Ruther answers, "I had to stop him. Besides, I was gentle."

Laar says sarcastically, "Is that why he's sprawled out on the floor?"

Ruther mumbles, "Do you have a better idea?"

Laar hints, "You could have simply restrained him."

Ruther gestures. "Forget it. It's done. Now what do we do with him? He's a blind stubborn fool. We can't bring him to Vendra."

Laar suggests, "Maybe we can leave him on a planet along the way. At least he'll be safe."

Ruther sighs. "This looks like the end of a long friendship. I'm sorry it had to end this way."

Chapter 14

End of The Realm

The Director speaks. "The Realm is on the verge of defeat. We had the power to resist the invasion if it had not been accompanied by the rebellion. The rebel army forced us to divert too much strength against it. We didn't have enough left to stop the invasion. We were fighting a war on two fronts, one of which was in the heart of The Realm. Every day brings news of another outer system that has surrendered. The fleets are being forced farther and farther apart. Retreating ships are falling prey to pirate attacks. It seems that every enemy of The Realm has joined forces to bring us down. I never realized such an alliance could ever be formed. The rebel force has beaten Realm forces soundly in several battles. They seem to do the impossible. They have overcome unbeatable odds, escaped from impossible situations, and penetrated fortresses that we thought impenetrable. They have small squadrons of superior ships. They outmaneuver our finest ships and dare to attack an entire fleet alone. They inflict heavy losses before retreating. We chase them until we run out of fuel, but they never seem to run out. Who are they?"

A guard announces, "Director, Brodis is here with someone."

The Director orders, "Send him in."

"Who is this, Brodis?"

Brodis replies, "This man calls himself Cholly. He was a Lander on Meris before the invasion. He has provided the answer that you require."

The Director bellows, "I need to know how we can save The Realm. Can you answer that?"

Brodis says, "He knows who the rebels are."

The Director snaps, "Who are they? Who is destroying The Realm?"

Cholly replies, "The Order of the Universe, Director."

The Director in disbelief replies, "The Order? How did they put together an army like this? And why? They have minded their own affairs all this time. Maybe they were building up to this from the start."

Cholly adds, "They blame The Realm for the dead solar systems in Cotalion."

The Director shouts, "How did they find out?"

Cholly yells, "Then it is true? You criminals!"

The Director commands, "Kill him, Brodis. Now we know who they are, but it is too late. I will get my revenge right now. Brodis, take our solar destruction device and plant it in Vendra's sun. We will decimate the membership of the Order and destroy their home planet. Go quickly. There is no time to waste. I should have known that only the Order could accomplish this. They have always defended themselves successfully against our attacks. I

144

should never allowed them to exist independently. I should have placed an embargo on them and starved them out. Now I have the means to destroy them, and I will. They may have defeated me, but I will destroy them in return. The Realm will take down its enemies with it."

***

The Trustee speaks. "You have done an excellent job in your prior missions. Now that the end for The Realm is near, I am asking you to perform one final mission."

Ruther says, "Name it. We're ready."

The Trustee advises, "The three of you must abduct the Director and Doctor Deemer. Bring them to Vendra to stand trial."

Ruther asks, "Do you have a plan?"

The Trustee affirms, "Yes. You will abduct the Director first. You will land without military detection on the capital planet. You will conceal the ship and take up temporary residence in the vicinity of the palace grounds. Teena will enter the palace and pass herself off as one of the director's mistresses. He has so many that the possibility of detection is remote. When the Director calls for a mistress, you will answer the call. You will render the Director unconscious and signal Laar and Ruther with a single transmission flash. The two of you will be disguised as servants and you will smuggle the Director into the kitchen under a food cart. Once in the kitchen, you will put the Director into the trash disposal. You will hijack a disposal vehicle and cart the canister to where your ship is. Once you have the Director, you will travel to the military research planet where Deemer is. Teena, you will convince your former companion master to help you. He was fond of you, wasn't he?"

Teena replies, "Yes, and he hates Deemer."

The Trustee continues, "Good. You should be able to get Doctor Deemer without much trouble then. If not, you will have to overcome the guards and take him by force.

"Go at once. Stay well."

Laar states, "Well, Teena. This time you will be commanding Deemer."

Teena replies, "I don't want revenge. I just want him where he cannot do harm to anyone else."

***

Iceman sneers, "Well, just look at that. Another lone pigeon. Down I go."

Brodis observes, "What's this? A ship approaching at intercept speed? I'd better evade it."

Iceman thinks, *So, he thinks he can run. He won't escape.*

Brodis ponders, *I'm being chased. I really don't have time to waste. I must get to the Vendrus System and complete my mission. But if it's a fight he wants, I'll give him one. It's probably one of the pirates that have been attacking our ships. I'll teach him a lesson.*

Iceman observes, *I think he's turning to fight. He's a live one. This will be fun. He has opened fire.*

"This is Brodis on an imperial mission. I suggest you heed my warning and back off. I am prepared to destroy your ship if need be."

Iceman mutters, "Brodis, I never thought I'd catch you out here alone."

Brodis demands, "Who are you? Identify yourself!"

Iceman replies, "It's only me, Brodis. Iceman."

Brodis responds, "Iceman! The Realm has been trying to put you out of business for a long time. It looks like I will have that singular pleasure."

Iceman challenges, "Well, Brodis. I accept your challenge. Kiss your life goodbye."

Brodis thinks, *I'll flank him just to see how he reacts.*

Iceman ponders, *He doesn't expect me to be outflanked does he?*

Brodice decides, *I'll dive at him and fire a cross barrage.*

Iceman reacts. *That was a bold maneuver. But now I'll chase.*

Brodis counters. *I'll spin and fire and then pull up.*

Iceman gathers himself. *That was too close. I underestimated Brodis. I'd better open fire just to give him something to think about.*

Brodis observes, *He's laying down a fire pattern to limit my options. This Iceman must have been trained at one of our military academies. Either that or he's a natural fighter. He's got an advantage. Time is on his side. I'm using up fuel fast. He probably has no trouble refueling on these outer planets now that The Realm is no longer in control. If I go down, I may meet up with rebels. I need to end this now.*

Iceman calculates, *He's zigzagging and looking for an opening. I'll give him one and close it fast.*

Brodis perceives, *He's baiting me. I'll take the bait and hope I guess right on his counterattack.*

Iceman readies himself. *He took the bait and is coming in. Now to stand firm and fire.*

Brodis prepares. *My guess is that he'll circle and attempt to flank me. Here I go. He stood firm! I'm wide open for a direct hit! No!*

Iceman gloats, "You were a challenge Brodis, but you outguessed yourself. You almost had me when you turned on me, but it was a matter of reflexes that saved me. You can count on reflexes. When it comes down to guessing though, it's anyone's game. I wasn't a better flier than Brodis, he just guessed wrong."

***

Teena quips, "We grabbed the Director without any problems."

Ruther replies, "Good job, Teena."

Teena continues, "It seems that the palace guards are a little out of practice. I guess nobody has attempted to harm the Director for quite some time. They aren't accustomed to trouble, and they aren't very alert."

Ruther adds, "Even so, it was a dangerous mission and it all depended on you, Teena. You handled it like a seasoned professional."

Teena suggests, "Well, let's concentrate on Deemer now. We should be receiving our landing instructions soon."

"This is Landing Control. Identify your ship and your purpose."

Laar responds, "This is *Ibex 2*. We are transporting an old friend of the Companion Master. She is here for a surprise visit."

Landing Control advises, "We will land you in Port 4. Do not attempt to disembark until you are cleared by the Master. We will put him through to your ship after you land. Follow our signal beam to land."

Laar says, "All right, Teena. It's in your hands again."

Teena states, "He will really be surprised."

"This is the Companion Master. To whom am I speaking?

Teena replies cheerfully, "Greetings, Master. It's Teena."

The Companion Master is surprised. "Teena! What are you doing here? You could get the both of us arrested."

Teena replies, "I only came for a short visit, Master. Aren't you happy that I'm here?"

The Companion Master responds, "I'm glad you're here, but you'd better wait there until I pick you up. I'll make sure nobody sees you. I've got to admit that this is a most pleasant surprise. Where are you?"

Teena replies, "We are in Port 4 in the *Ibex 2*. I am with two friends. You will be asked to clear us."

The Companion Master assures her, "Don't worry. I'll clear you and I'll see you in ten minutes."

Teena advises, "Everything is all right. He's coming to get us himself. No one will even know we're here. Put your suits on. He'll be here any minute. You'll like him. He's a gentle man."

Ruther asks, "Do you think he'll go along with us?"

Teens assures, "I know he won't expose us, and I think he'll help us just to rid himself of Deemer. Deemer is always injuring his girls and the Master is powerless to do anything about it. I'm sure now that he has a chance to do something, he will."

The lander announces, "The Companion Master is here to receive you."

The Companion Master is excited. "Teena! You've never looked better. I never thought I'd see you again. Teena, introduce me to your friends."

Teena gestures. "This is Ruther and Laar. I met Laar on Lexicon and Ruther is his partner."

The Companion Master leads. "Come. Let's get into my transport. We can talk on the way to my estate. What brings you here, Teena? This was very risky."

Teena replies, "We have urgent business here, Master."

The Companion Master inquires, "Business? Of what sort?"

Teena continues, "You are aware that Stasia is about to fall to Cotalion. Well, the reason for the invasion was invented right here."

The Companion Master is puzzled. "What do you mean?"

Teena continues, "Remember when Deemer molested me? Well, he ranted and raved about his new creation. The ultimate weapon. His weapon was used to destroy the solar systems that went dead in Cotalion."

The Companion Master cautiously asks, "Are you serious, Teena?"

Teens replies, "Yes. And now The Realm is being destroyed because of the atrocities it committed. We are here to abduct Deemer so that he can stand trial along with the Director for their crimes."

The Companion Master is surprised. "You are working for Cotalion? How did that come about?"

Teena answers, "When Ruther heard my story, he felt compelled to report it to the Order of the Universe."

The Companion Master admits, "I've heard of them, but don't know much about them."

Teena explains, "The Trustees heard our story and asked us to join the Order. They enlisted us to help them end The Realm threat to the universe. We joined and have been working with Cotalion to defeat The Realm."

The Companion Master states, "But, Teena, you sold out your whole galaxy. You must realize that we will be ruled by conquerors."

Teena advises, "The alternatives were carefully weighed and this was considered the best way to restore stability to the galaxy and preserve universal balance. We could not allow The Realm to have this new weapon and we needed to replace The Realm with another government that was powerful enough to control the galaxy. We did not want the galaxy to become a series of independent federations that would be engaged in constant power struggles. The Cotalions will keep the galaxy under control."

The Companion Master replies, "I have no stake in the outcome. I don't think anything will change here except that we will be working for a new authority. With Deemer gone, life will be easier for me and the companions. How do you intend to take Deemer?"

Teena answers, "I was hoping you would help. He has always been trouble for you."

The Companion Master asks, "How can I help?"

Teena replies, "Lure him here somehow, and we will do the rest."

The Companion Master relents. "I will try for the sake of the companions who rely on me. It is not easy to overlook his cruelty. I will be happy to be rid of him. But for now, let's enjoy your visit. I will get some refreshments. We have a lot to catch up on. It has been a long time."

***

A councilman announces, "The Director is gone. He has taken one of his mistresses and vanished. He knew the end was in sight and escaped while he could."

Another councilman responds, "That coward. Assemble the Cabinet. We must decide what to do."

The presiding councilman speaks. "Members of the Cabinet, we are faced with a new crisis. The Director has abdicated. It is up to us to decide the fate of The Realm. Please respond so that an attendance can be taken. Only six have not responded. We have a majority present. We have the power to act. You are all aware that our forces are near defeat. It is only a matter of time. Our choices are limited. We can continue to fight to the last outpost."

A councilman states, "That would only cause more casualties."

The presiding councilman continues, "We could summon our remaining forces and retreat to a designated sector in order to regroup and form a final front to defend against the Cotalions and hold them off indefinitely. If successful, we could preserve The Realm and rebuild again."

A councilman asks, "What is our chance of success? Thus far our efforts at defense have failed. What makes you think we can succeed this time?"

The presiding councilman replies, "If we regroup, we will not be faced with rebellion. That is what defeated us up to now."

A councilman counters, "But do we have enough strength remaining to stop a full-scale attack? And if so, will we be able to assemble them in time to form a defense perimeter before we are overwhelmed?"

The presiding councilman responds, "This is the question. Our only other alternative is surrender. If we surrender, The Realm is no more. We will be at the mercy of the Cotalions."

A councilman states, "It is a matter of lives now. I don't think we should resist any longer. Let us surrender and face the consequences. We can stop the suffering if we end this. Let us do what is best for our people. The Realm is dead. We cannot continue to serve a corpse."

The presiding councilman directs, "Let us put it to a vote. All in favor of regrouping, please respond. The tally is thirteen. All in favor of surrender, please respond. The tally is thirty-one. The decision is made. I will make arrangements for our immediate surrender. This will likely be our last meeting. Farewell."

***

Teena gestures. "Deemer, we meet again."

Doctor Deemer is surprised, "Teena! You told me she was dead. What is this?"

Teena smiles, "This time I am in command, Deemer. You will come with us."

Doctor Deemer resists. "No! I'm not going anywhere!"

Teena orders, "Take him. Thank you, Master. We must go now. We will meet again soon."

The Companion Master departs. "I hope so, Teena. Your visit was wonderful. I wish you and your friends the best. Stay well."

Teena replies, "You have done many favors for me. If there is something I can do for you in the future, just ask."

The cCompanion Master answers, "No. It is a master's job to look after his companions."

Teena says, "You have never failed me, Master. Stay well."

Ruther says, "Let's get back to Vendra. Get us into communication range as fast as you can Laar. I want to let the Trustees know that we succeeded."

***

The presiding councilman speaks. "I am the spokesman for the Cabinet of The Realm. The Director has abdicated. I am authorized to surrender to you immediately. Please allow our ships to return to their nearest bases at which time, the bases will be surrendered to you."

Admiral Tele is jubilant. "This is Admiral Tele. We accept your surrender. Your troops will be treated with the proper consideration due prisoners of war. A military dictatorship will be formed as the temporary authority over your galaxy. Signal your forces and advise them of your surrender. This is your last communication in an official capacity. You are now relieved of all authority. Your Cabinet members and you are to assemble in the palace and await my arrival. You will then be interrogated and set free to go your own ways.

"This is Admiral Tele to all commanders. The enemy has surrendered. We will form a military government as soon as the occupation is complete. Let us drink to victory."

Admiral Tele orders, "Contact our allies. Advise them of the surrender. Have their leaders meet me at the palace. We can then discuss their wishes."

The attendant speaks. "Admiral, the Trustees wish to speak with you."

Admiral Tele blurts, "Connect me."

The Trustee speaks joyfully. "Congratulations on your overwhelming victory, Admiral Tele."

Admiral Tele acknowledges him. "Thank you."

The Trustee continues, "We have some good news for you as well. Our members have the Dictator and the inventor of the device in their custody. They are bringing them to Vendra to stand trial. Since we never leave Vendra, we will send Teena, Laar, and Ruther to your meeting as representatives. As soon as they return, we will request your presence at the trial. We feel Cotalion should have a part in the proceedings to give it legality. After your meeting, Teena, Laar, and Ruther will return to Vendra. You may wish to accompany them. We will postpone the trial until your arrival. Is it agreed?"

Admiral Tele concurs. "Agreed. I will await your representatives."

***

A guard announces, "Admiral Tele, the representatives are here."

Admiral Tele commands, "Have them wait in the study. I'll join them presently."

The guard advises, "The Admiral will be right in. Make yourselves comfortable."

Admiral Tele arrives. "Sorry to keep you. I called you here to discuss your wishes now that the war is over. We have set up a temporary military government pending the outcome of this meeting and final orders from the High Council. What is your position?"

Laar speaks, "The order wishes no concessions. We want only to act as outside observers and advisors. The organization and administration of Stasia will be left to you. All that we ask is that we have a hand in the planning so that we can ensure that balance is restored, and that no new threat to universal is created."

Admiral Tele responds, "Your wishes will be conveyed to the High Council. If you have nothing more to say, we will adjourn this meeting. Tomorrow, I will accompany you to Vendra. My orderly will get you whatever you wish. Enjoy your stay."

***

The judge declares, "The trial of the Director and Doctor Deemer will now commence. The charges are as follows:

"The Director is charged with ordering the destruction of nine solar systems in the Cotalion Galaxy. This carries additional charges of mass murder, interference with the economy of a galaxy, and disruption of universal balance.

"Doctor Deemer is charged with creating a device with the sole purpose of planetary destruction. He is also charged with irresponsibility in the control of a potentially cataclysmal device. He is further charged with concealing knowledge of a crime and participating in its commission. Finally, he is charged with the brutal torture and maiming of several companions on the science planet, one of whom is present here today."

The prosecutor asks, "Director, do you have any response to the charges leveled against you?"

The Director responds defiantly, "I don't recognize this court, and will not answer to it."

The prosecutor warns, "You will be subject to the decision of this court. Your recognition has no bearing."

The director continues, "You have no authority. You are nothing more than vigilantes."

The prosecutor asks, "Doctor Deemer, do you have any response?"

Doctor Deemer states, "I created a weapon for the defense of The Realm. As a defense scientist, it was my job. I had no idea that it would be used in any other manner. It was a doomsday device in case our galaxy was destroyed. In my mind, strictly a retaliatory weapon. I thought it could be used to prevent a galactic conflict. I never expected it to be used as it was."

The prosecutor chastises, "You should never have created such a device or allowed its plans to leave your lab. The plans should have been destroyed for the good of the universe. You cannot be permitted to practice this brand of science. It is far too dangerous. You as a scientist should know that.

The prosecutor continues, "Do you have anything else to add to your statement?"

Doctor Deemer continues, "I didn't harm the companions. Their job is to provide pleasure. I simply took my pleasure. If I violated the code of behavior, why wasn't I stopped?"

The prosecutor further states, "You were protected by the Director and permitted to do whatever you chose as a reward for creating the device. Anyone else would have been disciplined. You treated those girls as if you had the right to abuse them, even to the point of permanently injuring them. You committed your own brand of atrocities on the companions. They were forced beyond their required duties. You took pleasure in torture. It is barbaric and inhuman."

Doctor Deemer declares, "I am not guilty! I did nothing wrong! I am innocent! Set me free! Please!"

The judge speaks. "This court will now deliberate. Take the prisoners until we call for them."

The prosecutor speaks, "First, we will decide the verdict of the Director. The charges against him are of the gravest nature. Do we all agree to his guilt on all charges?"

The jury in unison shouts, "Guilty!"

The judge speaks. "We must devise a punishment suitable for his crimes."

The prosecutor replies, "There is no place in the universe for such a creature. He cannot be allowed to live. He is a most vile monster. All traces of his being should be eradicated."

The judge asks, "Do we all agree? So be it. He will be executed, and his body burned. His ashes will be dumped on one of the dead suns that he extinguished."

"Now for Doctor Deemer."

The prosecutor states, "I suggest the same for him. Let him be deposited on one of the places he destroyed. Let him become part of the results of his creation."

The judge inquires, "Are we all in agreement? Very well."

"Send the prisoners in for sentencing."

The judge continues, "You have both been found guilty of all charges levelled against you. Your sentences will be carried out.

"Director, it has been decided that your crimes are so vile that there is no place for you in the Universe. Since matter cannot be destroyed, you will be executed and your body reduced to ashes. The remaining ashes will be dumped on one of the suns you destroyed. Your memory will die there.

"Doctor Deemer, your life has brought misery and suffering to countless others. Your work created destruction rather than growth. You will be executed and burned. Your ashes will be dumped on one of the suns destroyed by your device. In death you will become part of your own creation. You have built your own tomb.

"Take the prisoners away to be executed."

Admiral Tele speaks. "I will relay the outcome of the trial to the High Council. I must take my leave now. There is much to be done. I will be in contact as events unfold."

The Trustee declares, "It is now the responsibility of the Order of the Universe to see to it that Stasia is structured in a manner that will promote stability. We took the responsibility of dissolving The Realm. Now we are responsible for its replacement."